Lonen's Reign

Sorcerous Moons – Book 6

BY

JEFFE KENNEDY

This book was previously published with a different cover

A LOOMING THREAT

The sorceress Oria has finally come into her own—able to wield the power of her birthright and secure in the marriage she once believed would bring her only misery. But the past she escaped still chases her, and the certainty of war promises to destroy everything she's fought to have.

AN IMPOSSIBLE WAR

Once before Lonen led an army in a desperate attempt to stop the powerfully murderous sorcerers of Bára—and he nearly lost everything. Now he must return to the battlefield that took the lives of so many of his people. Only this time he has more to risk than ever.

THE FINAL CONFLICT

With guile, determination—and unexpected allies—Oria and Lonen return to the place where it all began… and only hope that it won't also be the end of them.

DEDICATION

For Rebecca Cremonese,
Who gave so much attention and care to every little detail.

Acknowledgements

Many thanks to Jim Sorenson and Sage Walker, for encouraging me to persevere and finish this series. And for Sunday brunches and wide-ranging conversations.

A special thank you to Carien, for fact-checking and asking the right questions. And for being there for all these years. Just amazing, isn't it?

Huge thanks, too, to all of you who commented on the podcasts and blog posts, and in the private group, who cheered me on and have been waiting for this conclusion. I hope it's the grand finale you wished for.

Love to Kelly Robson for daily chats, hearts and kisses. Also to Cathy Smith for the same. And to my mom for being a patron of the arts.

And always to David, who loves me just the way I am.

Thank you for reading!

<u>Credits</u>
Line and Copy Editor: Rebecca Cremonese
Cover Design: Arel B. Grant, BZN Studio Designs

~ 1 ~

"Just a few more moments of your patience, Your Highness," the healer Baeltya said, her tone abstracted as she concentrated.

Lonen stared up at the patterned, arched ceiling of Arill's Temple, counting the interweaving strips of wood yet again. There were one thousand and fifty-two in the central spiral. He should be grateful for Arill's magic—and Her dedicated priestesses who devoted themselves to healing—which made convalescence so much faster, if profoundly uncomfortable. Mostly, however, he chafed at the enforced inactivity. Much easier not to get injured in the first place.

At least his mother, who'd initially taken care of the gut wound he'd received from his brother Nolan during their duel, had left the follow-up care to Baeltya. The junior healer didn't lecture him the way Vycayla, as both the dowager queen and his mother, seemed to feel entitled to do. Not only entitled, but compelled.

If he didn't need her help to ensure he and Oria could officially marry with Arill's blessing, according to Destrye law, he'd be tempted to tell his mother to go back to her hermitage already.

The wedding ceremony was a stupid formality, really. With the duel over and Lonen's claim to the throne of Dru secured, he could declare Oria his wife and Queen of the Destrye once and for all. They'd fought hard enough for it. It still stuck in his craw that he'd had to fight his brother for it.

"Try not to twitch, Your Highess," Baeltya said, sounding more emphatic and less vague. "This is a delicate piece."

"I wouldn't want you to meld my intestines to my bladder after all," he commented wryly.

"You laugh, but given the previous state of your intestines, that's not impossible," she replied in a tart tone, her healing magic twisting in parts of his gut he wished he didn't know about. "That final blow could've killed you—likely would've killed a man in less robust condition—so maybe spend this time contemplating your gratitude to Arill for Her healing gifts."

"I'm grateful," he grumbled. Though he'd much rather be with Oria and his mother as they sorted through Nolan's psyche. He couldn't decide if it made him feel better or worse that Nolan's rebellion and treachery might have been fueled by a sorcerous taint from his time in Bára. And Arnon... Lonen didn't know what to make of his younger brother's changeable loyalty. First Arnon had backed Nolan's challenge, then—apparently somehow swayed by their mother Vycayla's return from self-imposed exile—he had refused to act as Nolan's second.

So ironic that they accused Lonen of being enchanted and duped by his sorceress wife to the point they questioned his devotion to Dru, and now Oria was the only person he felt he could fully trust.

He sighed heavily.

"Your Highness..."

"That was a sigh, not a twitch."

She laughed. "I don't envy Oria in managing you if you're

always this difficult."

"She has other ways of managing me than chiding complaints." Which only reminded him that they could touch now. He could finally and truly bed his beautiful sorceress—and he'd instead been laid up for two days recovering. "Will I be well enough to be released after this?"

"In a hurry to leave us? We'll see. Queen Vycayla will have the final word."

"Wonderful," he muttered.

As if evoked by her name, Vycayla swept into the room, asking Baeltya for a report and not bothering to greet her son at all. With determined resignation, Lonen resumed counting the ceiling pieces and waited for them to conclude their healer conversation. He'd learned better than to interrupt, as it only delayed them, extended his involuntary stay, and earned his mother's scathing remarks about what he didn't know. That's what being king got you—no power in your own household.

His mother laid a hand on his brow, not a soothing maternal gesture but testing his vitality for herself. Her serious gray eyes looked through him, large in her severe face. She didn't show her age much in wrinkles, but time had pared away any trace of youthful softness. With her long hair tightly braided back, her bones seemed to show through translucent skin. She raised a brow at his appraisal. "You're much improved, my impetuous son."

"Improved enough to have the wedding?" he asked. He would've preferred to sit up and have this conversation at least upright if they wouldn't let him stand, but he'd have to fight them both and he'd lose.

"Yes." They both murmured reprimands, gentle hands restraining him as he nearly leapt for freedom. "*Not* this exact moment," his mother added with a hint of a smile. "But we can set a date and plan the ceremony."

"The ceremony will be tonight," he said, using a tone of authority.

His mother rolled her eyes. "You're not some timber brat marrying a milkmaid. This is an event. The King of Dru is marrying a Princess of Bára, who will become Queen of the Destrye. You will be joining two realms that have been at war for centuries. It must be done with appropriate pomp and celebration."

Lonen set his teeth. "No, I'm not marrying a milkmaid. I'm marrying a woman who is already my wife and has been for the better part of a year."

"You didn't marry her under Arill's hand," his mother corrected.

"I *know* that," he replied as evenly as possible. "Which is why we're getting married *again*."

"Don't use that tone with me, boy," his mother snapped. "You're not too big to be turned over my knee and paddled."

Baeltya choked back a laugh. Since Lonen likely out-weighed his mother by twice as much, and most of it brawn, that assertion was ridiculous. Never mind the fact that he outranked her. Still… "Yes, Mother," he said with exaggerated deference.

"Better." She patted his cheek smartly enough to sting. "I shall perform the prayers to Arill to determine the most auspicious date and time for—"

Lonen wrapped a hand around her slender wrist, the bones spider-light. "I'm not waiting until spring or some such," he warned.

She relented, smiling with more warmth. "I agree. This is best handled speedily. I'll seek the most auspicious time in the next several weeks."

"Days."

Her smile faded. "Don't tell me my business, boy. I follow Arill's will, not yours—and no crown changes that."

He winced, and Vycayla echoed it, realizing the image she'd evoked. Nolan had been wearing the crown—a wreath of bronzed oak leaves—during the duel. When Lonen had brought the iron battle-axe down on his skull in a desperate move, with his brother's sword already spearing his gut, the leaves had cut Nolan's scalp.

Blood on the crown of Dru. Lonen couldn't shake the sight of it—or the lingering dread that it might be a terrible omen.

"How is he?" he asked quietly.

"Physically he's healed," Vycayla replied with crisp authority. Then shook her head. "Mentally, well… whatever stain they put on him, the iron of your axe only temporarily dimmed it. He's back to his vitriol and ranting. Oria is working on the problem."

"I still think a tincture of iron solution would work," Baeltya commented.

"If it doesn't poison him beyond retrieval," Vycayla replied dryly.

"There, Your Highness." Baeltya dusted her hands together to disperse the healing magic and any remanence lingering from her connection with him. "You may sit up."

At last. He sat up, vigor coursing through him. "Thank you. Both of you. I feel like a new man." He stood, brimming with a feverish excitement, pumped his arms and stomped his legs. "Where is Oria?"

"With Nolan in the dungeon," his mother said, then narrowed her eyes. "Why?"

"I intend to see my wife," he answered blandly. And he intended to take Oria to bed and at last fuck her properly, until they both couldn't see straight. His balls grew heavy in anticipation. This long-delayed consummation would be sweet indeed. Maybe he'd keep her naked and in bed with him until the wedding and they could—

"You are not to be with Oria unchaperoned until the wedding night," his mother informed him, as if reading his thoughts.

Lonen paused in the midst of pulling on his shirt. "Excuse me?"

Vycayla drew herself up to her imposing height, slight of build, eyes of steel. "You can sound as dangerous as you like, but you *will* heed me as high priestess of Arill's Temple. This wedding will be done properly. Oria's previous illness is well known, as is the fact that she's a virgin."

"Not so much," he answered with a feral grin. "In fact, we've—"

Vycayla held up a hand. "Spare me the details. So far as the physical consummation of your marriage in a child-engendering act, she is a virgin. And she will retain that state until you are properly married under Arill's hand."

He nearly sputtered as he fumed. "That has never been a Destrye requirement, that a bride be a virgin."

"Yes and no." Vycayla's eyes glittered. "The most sacred of Arill's binding ceremonies are at their most powerful with a woman whose body remains entirely female, who has never taken male flesh inside her."

"Oh, I've been inside her." Fingers, sure, but those counted as male flesh.

"Skin to skin?" Vycayla inquired archly. "Oria says you used gloves and other implements."

Abruptly, self-consciousness swamped him, to be having this conversation with his *mother*—while Baeltya stood by, dark eyes dancing in salacious amusement, though she kept a straight face. "I can't believe you asked Oria about this." Or that Oria had told her.

Vycayla raised her eyes to the heavens, lips moving in a silent prayer. "She will be my daughter. Women discuss these things. And I needed to know, for the ceremony. Arill has chosen wisely for you and we will honor Her hand in this by binding you in Her most sacred ceremony—one that will banish all the bad omens and taint from your kingship and marriage, and that will auger well for the Destrye in the battle to come. This is about more than you and your sexual urges. Do you understand now?" she asked, spacing out the words as if he were still a boy.

He scowled at her. "I greatly regret digging you out of your hermitage."

She smiled serenely. "As does Nolan. You're welcome. Will you abide by this, Your Highness?"

Oh, *now* she used the honorific. "I don't like it."

"You don't have to like it. You must simply agree."

"Don't make me wait too long, Mother."

She patted him on the cheek, gently, pleased with his capitulation. "You've waited all this time. What's a few more weeks?"

"Days."

"We'll see."

He'd been hearing that line since he was a boy, too—and it never boded well.

FINALLY FULLY DRESSED, battle-axe sheathed on his back, Lonen strode out of Arill's healing center in the temple. Baeltya walked along with him, hands folded neatly into the billowing embroidered cuffs of her deep green robes. Everyone they passed bowed to him, crying out their good wishes and joy at his return, an elaborate demonstration of fervent loyalty.

"You'd think they hadn't been bowing and scraping to my brother the usurper only days ago," he muttered under his breath.

"It was an incredibly difficult week," Baeltya replied quietly. "Nolan employed brutal methods to ensure the appearance of loyalty to his claim. Not that I'd expect you to thank him, but he has done you the favor of making the prospect of your reign look very good by comparison. These people are sincere in their delight—and relief."

A group of approaching Destrye warriors spotted him and all went to one knee, bowing their heads and saluting. "All hail His Highness King Lonen!"

They did sound sincere, holding the knee until he'd completely passed. He and Baeltya continued through the dark halls of the palace. Not a beautiful place, but a secure one, it had started out as a fortress, built upon by generations of Destrye and their kings. And with a warren of tunnels hollowed out below. The stairs took them down, past the food storage cellars, and Lonen didn't let his gaze linger on how meager those stores had become. A few more months before the first crops would be ripe, though perhaps Arill would bless them with an early spring.

Perhaps Oria could wield her sorcery to hasten the harvest.

Down another level and they passed the guards—also happy to greet him and congratulate his good health—and into the area used for prisoners. This deep, the earthen walls loomed dark, the great roots of the forest occasionally surfacing like the coil of a sea serpent before disappearing again. For a people accustomed to being outdoors, to climbing the trees of their home, the dungeons imposed their own punishment. Most Destrye chose death over imprisonment.

Nolan, however, would not be offered that option. Not yet.

He paced in a large cell at the end of the tunnel, fenced in by iron bars. Ranting and raving, indeed. His voice echoed down the narrow space, by turns cajoling and ordering. Oria sat very still on a wooden stool well out of reach, facing Nolan. She had her back to the hall, her exotic copper hair caught the torchlight, falling in a straight sheet like polished metal.

Knowing his sorceress, that she'd likely fallen into a deep meditative state as she used her magic, Lonen called out so as not to startle her. "Oria."

She spun on the stool, hair fanning with the movement, her lovely face full of delighted surprise. Running to him, she flew into his arms, a cloud of silk, spicy qinn, and luscious woman. He kissed her thoroughly, feeling he could never get enough of the feel and taste of her mouth, the way she fit against him.

"They let you out," Oria exclaimed when he let her come up for air. "It's so good to see you up." She'd been to visit him regularly while he was laid up healing, but she sounded as if she hadn't seen him in ages. Though they had been separated before their all-too-brief reunion and had no time at all to savor their ability to truly touch.

He ran his hands over her body, ignoring Nolan's crazed shouting and Baeltya's more discreet presence. "I should've taken you into that farmhouse," he growled in Oria's ear, taking the lobe of her ear into his mouth, biting lightly and then sucking on her deliciously sweet skin. She moaned softly, melting against him.

"But look how well everything turned out because you didn't," she answered, pulling back to give him a smile, her copper eyes wide and sparkling, the same color as her hair. "You're the undisputed King of the Destrye and—"

"I dispute it!" Nolan shouted.

"—we'll be married soon," Oria talked over his mad brother.

"Not soon enough," Lonen said, trailing his fingers over her satin cheek, down the swanlike column of her throat.

"Ah, they told you."

"Yes." He lowered his brows threateningly, though his scowl did nothing to dim her radiant smile. "You might've warned me on one of your visits."

She lifted onto her toes and kissed him. "I didn't want to upset you. It will be only a short wait. All is falling into place. Especially now that you're healed."

"Come in here and I'll cut you open again!" Nolan practically screamed. He had his hands wrapped around the iron bars, fisted as he shook them.

With a sigh, Lonen tucked Oria against his side, at least savoring her closeness under his arm. She nestled against him, both of them watching Nolan as he flung himself against the bars, hurtling threats like a tree monkey flinging feces—filthy but without much effect.

"What have you discovered?" he asked Oria.

She shook her head slightly. "The enchantment is there, but it's… slippery. I can't think of a better way to describe it. I can sense it, get near, then it's gone before I can get a good look at it."

"Maybe you need a break," he suggested.

She glanced up with an arch expression. "We can't—"

"Not that," he interrupted. "Is sex all you think about?"

Gratifyingly, she giggled. He ignored Baeltya's snicker. "Let's get out of this hole," he said. "I've been cooped up for days and I want to be outside, to see the sky."

Oria's face lit up. "Would you like to fly? Chuffta says he'd like to."

Her winged lizard Familiar—now a dragon the size of Arill's Temple—likely put it more emphatically. Flying sounded perfect. He hadn't been able to enjoy it the one time before, carrying the injured Alyx between him and Oria during their swift trip to make it in time for his duel with Nolan.

"I would like that." He ran a hand over Oria's hip, contemplating what he might do to her.

Baeltya cleared her throat.

"Oh, brother." Lonen fixed the healer with a baleful glare. "What could we get up to on dragonback?"

Baeltya raised her elegant brows. "If you need me to explain that, Your Highness…"

"You can come with us," Oria invited, slanting him a quelling look. "If you'd like to, that is."

Baeltya's face transformed with rapture. "Truly?" she breathed. "I'd *love* to fly."

"A threesome it is," Lonen declared, just to laugh at their outrage. "Come along, ladies. I'm ready for fresh air."

And they left his treacherous brother shouting his rage behind them.

~ 2 ~

"**W**HAT IS TAKING *so looonnnnngggg?*" Chuffta dragged out the question on an exaggerated moan of his mind-voice. Though Oria couldn't see him—as they had yet to leave the palace—she felt him impatiently furling and unfurling his wings, dancing in place and lashing his tail. She didn't know if she felt his body movements so vividly now because of his greatly enhanced size making every sensation larger, or because her magic had linked them more tightly when she'd used it to make him big.

"Don't hit anything," she cautioned him silently. Like a wolfhound pup grown too fast, Chuffta had yet to fully comprehend his new size and how his body occupied space. Something crashed behind Chuffta and she felt him mentally wince.

"Oops. But the Destrye have lots more trees."

She sighed. Hearing it, Lonen raised a brow at her as he waved away the cluster of attendants and helped Oria into the shadowcat fur cloak himself. She shook her head minutely, unwilling to explain with so many ears to hear. The Destrye in general didn't know the extent of her and Chuffta's abilities, and she preferred it that way for the time being. Lonen had originally insisted upon it and she'd grown to appreciate his discretion. Who knew what would come in useful in the months of war to come? Her brother Yar might have created more spies than Nolan from the men in his regiment who had emerged from the lake under Bára.

Until the palace guard had all those men quietly rounded up for her to examine, Oria had been focusing her attention on sorting through Nolan's chaotic and vengeful thoughts. Now that Lonen had emerged from the healers' care, he'd likely be expediting the containment of the possible spies. She would study them, of course, but she didn't know what more she'd find out from many minds that she couldn't dig out of one. Especially when that one had been the primary target of whatever Yar and his cohorts had done. That was something that continued to elude her. She might have her power back— and finally the ability to manage it—but she couldn't match the centuries of accumulated knowledge Yar had at his command in the temples at Bára.

"Are you mad at me?" Chuffta asked the question meekly and she realized she'd been too deep in thought to reply to him. Another change with her improved control: she shielded so well that Chuffta no longer "heard" her surface thoughts unless she directed them mentally.

"We're on our way," she reassured Chuffta. *"We had to stop for warm gear. It's winter and even colder in the air. And we have to walk to where you are."*

"I miss being in the same place as you." Chuffta sounded a little forlorn, and lonely. *"I didn't know I'd miss riding around on your shoulder. Remember how I'd twine my tail around your arm?"*

Yes, because it had been only a couple of weeks before, but she kept the amusement out of her mind-voice. Derkesthai had a different perception of time, and Chuffta was a young member of a long-lived race. That hadn't changed just because he'd grown huge. *"I miss having you close, too."*

She really did. Sleeping alone in Lonen's big bed while he recovered had made her realize she hadn't been entirely without company since she was seven—except for those horrible few days when Head Healer Talya had isolated her in an attempt to "save" Lonen from her enchantment. It would have been a great comfort to feel Chuffta's solid little body curled up against her. A price for everything, she supposed. Chuffta had wanted to be big—and she'd wanted it for him—and neither of them had given thought to how that would separate them.

The problem was, the way the solid fortress that was the Destrye palace sat at the base of the immense tree that housed Arill's Temple, a winged creature of Chuffta's size couldn't easily approach. Even if they cleared a flight path for him, there was nowhere for him to land. The Destrye used every handspan of ground inside the moat around the city to keep out the Báran golems.

The haphazard shelters piled up around the palace and temple grounds like sands blown into dunes against city walls, and even the pathways between them were so narrow in places that she, Lonen, and Baeltya had to sometimes go single file as they walked out to cross the moat and meet Chuffta. The Destrye, glimpsing their king, cheered and bowed—and quickly cleared the way—but it was slow going.

"How can it be taking so long?" Chuffta demanded.

"Where *is* Chuffta?" Lonen asked at the same time, his disgruntled tone so like her Familiar's that she had to laugh.

"Outside the moat," she explained, waving forgiveness to a woman who babbled apologies as she pushed a cart full of wood out of their way. Oria raised a brow at Lonen's incredulous expression and gestured at the crush. "Where else did you think we'd put him?"

"I hadn't thought," he admitted. "I'm so used to having him always right there."

"*See?*" Chuffta said, pouncing on the words as if they proved his point. "*I should be with you. All the time.*"

"I don't know where else he'd fit," she explained to them both in some exasperation.

"Isn't he cold outside?" Lonen furrowed his brow in concern.

"*Yes. I'm cold allll the time.*"

Oria mentally rolled her eyes at him. "He's fine. He generates so much heat at his size that he can't get cold."

"*Easy for you to say.*"

"That's not fair to Chuffta," Lonen pointed out. "You know how he loves to sleep by the fire."

"*Right! This is not fair to me, Oria.*"

Oria harnessed her impatience with both of her boys. "Where inside is big enough to put him?" They'd emerged from the warren of shelters that blocked the sky and stood poised on the edge of the wide moat while guards jumped to extend the bridge for them to cross. Chuffta stood on the other rim, tail lashing, his white scales iridescent in the winter light, gleaming where the surrounding snow glittered. He curved his neck in coy welcome, his triangular head elegant and green eyes bright as small suns.

"Holy Arill," Lonen breathed. "I'd somehow not entirely absorbed how truly huge he is now."

"He may have gotten bigger," Oria admitted. Not that she'd worked any magic to do it, but he seemed larger to her eyes, too. Perhaps he was just filling out, like a quickly growing adolescent boy getting his height first, then packing on muscle.

"He's beautiful," Baeltya said in reverent tones. "I mean,

you were always a handsome creature, Chuffta, but now you are a true wonder."

He preened, happy to hear Baeltya's words. The healer was one of the few to understand the depth of the bond—and clarity of communication—between Oria and her Familiar. Where other Destrye regarded him as a pet, or even an animal companion with the childlike intelligence of a warhorse or wolfhound, Baeltya grasped how much Chuffta understood their words.

"He appreciates your praise," Oria murmured. "But temper that, as his head has clearly swelled to gigantic proportions as it is."

"Hey! I am perfectly proportioned, thank you—and thanks to you."

Crowds of Destrye had gathered to observe him, and Oria worried that the press might end with some of them pitching into the moat. Dry and deep, the moat held an array of sharpened wooden and iron stakes. In their mindless advances, the golems would fall in and impale themselves, the only sure defense the Destrye had been able to find against the Báran's puppet monsters. Short of chopping the golems to pieces with iron weapons, which exacted as great a toll on the fighter as the golem.

The guards finished extending the bridge—a clever contraption of wooden planks that could be rolled or unrolled with a system of pulleys—and the three of them crossed. Lonen frowned thoughtfully up at Chuffta, assessing him. "What if we built another level on the palace with a roof platform large and strong enough for Chuffta to land on?"

"Yes! Yes yes yes yes."

"Can you do that?"

Lonen gave her an arch look. "I *am* king. I'm reliably informed I can do whatever I want to." His gaze went to her mouth, lingering there as he considered what he wanted to do but couldn't, lust firing hot in his mind—along with the image of her naked and under him. She had to close out his thoughts. The wedding couldn't happen soon enough.

"I meant," she replied in a deliberately prim tone, intended to cool his ardor, "is it possible to do that?"

"The structure is solid enough to bear the weight," he replied, considering, mentally measuring Chuffta as they approached. "We'd have to clear some limbs, but we could put that wood to good use in the construction. We could build a set of apartments there for our rooms—with lots of windows, a balcony for you, and a rooftop garden for summer if you like."

Her heart clutched, her steps slowing. "You've been thinking about this."

"Of course," he replied absently, then looked down at her, his granite gray eyes clear and full of love. "I promised you long ago that I'd do everything to make you happy here in Dru, to give you as much of what you left behind in Bára as I could. I've been mulling for a long time how to give you a balcony and garden again like—"

She flung herself against him, cutting off his words with a kiss.

"*Can't you kiss your mate later?*" Chuffta asked plaintively. "*After all, you can do* that *when you're inside.*"

Laughing, she broke the kiss. "Chuffta is impatient."

Lonen gave Chuffta—whose head hovered barely above theirs, his breath hot as a furnace—a baleful stare. "There are words for this kind of behavior, Chuffta man."

Chuffta grumbled in Oria's mind and backed off a bit. Baeltya coughed politely from a discreet distance away—

though not so far that they could forget the strictures against them doing more than kissing.

"When *is* the wedding?" Oria breathed.

His hands tightened on her. "I'll have an answer when we return, one way or another." His mouth fastened on hers, hot and luxuriant, full of promises. She melted into it, savoring the sweetness of being *with* him. Their separation had felt like an eternity, and they'd had no time since to just be together. In that moment, she could regret that she hadn't taken him up on the offer to run off into the hills with him, that she'd insisted he reclaim the throne. "I swear to Arill," he muttered against her mouth, "if it's more than three days from now, I'm taking you captive, tossing you over Buttercup's back, and escaping somewhere I can ravage you at my leisure."

"You wouldn't have to," she answered. "I'd go willingly."

"Yes, but my way is more fun," he said, the wickedly sensual gleam in his eyes making them glint with silvery light. "Let's ride Chuffta into the sunset right now."

"It's still morning," she pointed out.

"Details."

"And there's our chaperone."

"We can toss Baeltya into the moat."

"I heard that," Baeltya said in a clear voice, a ripple of laughter in it.

Lonen heaved a heavy sigh and let go of Oria. "All right then, I suppose flying will be fun, too."

IT WAS, AND more glorious than she'd ever imagined before she could ride on Chuffta's back. Even before, when she rode along in his thoughts as he flew, it hadn't felt the same—the stomach-dropping dives, and heart-pounding ascents, the rush of chill air stinging her cheeks and Lonen's arms strong around her as she sat cradled between his muscled thighs. Baeltya sat discreetly behind him, circumspect but for the occasional startled squeak when Chuffta did something unexpected.

Between Lonen's proximity and Chuffta's mind filling hers, Oria let both of their thoughts and emotions stream through her like the wind of their passage, like the midday sun hot on her eyelids when she closed them, and the dazzling panorama of the forests of Dru beneath them when she looked. In the distance, white-capped mountains reared against a sizzling blue sky. Somewhere in those peaks, Chuffta's derkesthai kin lived in a colony deep inside a volcanic cavern.

"I'd like to go back someday," Chuffta said, picking up on her thoughts now, with her shields so fully open. *"When we're done with war."*

"Is that not where you were hatched?" she asked. They'd had little time to discuss the colony and what had happened to them there. Also, she'd been hesitant to ask, feeling an odd sense of intruding on something she shouldn't.

"Oh, no. Though I don't remember that much about before I was your Familiar. That's why it would be fun to go back and see those derkesthai, so I can spend time there awake!"

Guilt assailed her, that she'd misused her magic so badly that she'd nearly killed her Familiar. Then the moment she managed to bring him out of the deep sleep she'd put him in, they'd raced away to find Lonen. *"I'm so sorry, my friend."*

"A mistake only—and one that led to good things. You mastered your sorcery, all because of me."

He sounded so proud that she had to smile despite the

agonizing regret. *"I think 'mastered' is a bit of a stretch."*

"You made me big. No sorcerer or sorceress has done that in generations. We will be famous! They'll write history books about us."

"Hopefully those tales won't include a tragic ending where we die a fiery death on the battlefield," she commented wryly.

"They won't. We shall be triumphant!" He tossed his head and let out a bugling roar, complete with green flame—which blew back on his passengers, who all ducked with cries of dismay.

"Oops. Sorry."

"Something else to practice," she noted without rancor. She could hardly hold such mistakes against him when she'd committed far worse ones.

"THAT WAS THE most incredible experience of my entire life," Baeltya gushed as they waited at the edge of the moat for the guards to extend the bridge. She turned and curtsied deeply to Chuffta, who returned the gesture with a dramatic sweep of wings. "Thank you, sir, for the lovely treat."

"Tell her I'm sorry about the flame backfire."

Oria relayed that remark and Baeltya laughed. "I can only imagine how much practice that sort of thing takes."

"Speaking of which," Oria said to Lonen. "I'd like to spend time each day practicing riding Chuffta."

He frowned at her. "Chuffta can practice his flaming and flying without you. We need you working on the corruption in Nolan's mind and his men's."

"Three things," she replied. "First, Nolan's men haven't all been located and confined, and I haven't been given access to the ones that have. Second—" She raised her brows at him when he opened his mouth to interrupt, and he closed it again, with exaggerated patience. "Second, I can only spend so much time in Nolan's mind before I need to clear my own head. Third, I need to practice working magic from Chuffta's back as he flies, coordinating mentally with him so that we can do that in battle, if necessary."

His frown deepened. "You're proposing… riding Chuffta into battle, against Bára?"

"Were you planning to leave me at home?" she asked sweetly.

Lonen's expression went carefully blank, his gaze opaque as he scrambled to collect his thoughts. Feeling no compunction, Oria peeked at the stream of them and found him hastily readjusting his assumptions. He *had* somehow envisioned her remaining in Dru, safe from harm in the mighty forests, but he realized Oria wouldn't be able to work her sorcery from so far away, and they'd need her at Bára, as she knew the city and the people. He would learn from his father's mistakes and not risk alienating his beloved wife by ordering her to stay clear of battle. And he'd promised Alyx and the women warriors that he'd change the laws prohibiting women from fighting alongside the men.

He didn't like it… but the course ahead became clear. "Of course you should practice on Chuffta, love," he said, running a hand over her hair. "I wasn't thinking clearly."

Fascinating, to see his sharp mind in action. She smiled, pleased with the result. The bridge reached them, and the three of them crossed over.

"I'm off to find my mother," Lonen told her as they

reached the palace entrance, the guards snapping to attention. "Would you like to come along?"

Oria shook her head. She didn't dislike Vycayla, but the dowager queen could be sharp—and not a little intimidating—and as mother to Nolan as well as Lonen, she'd no doubt have questions about Nolan's mental health. Questions Oria had no intention of trying to answer yet.

"No, I think I'll go work with Nolan some more. I'll see you at dinner?"

"How about a private dinner, in our rooms?" Lonen suggested with a salacious smile—and a vivid image of dribbling wine over her naked breasts.

Oria felt her cheeks heat and Baeltya cleared her throat. "Your Highness, please don't make me get stern with you."

"It would be just dinner," Lonen claimed in innocent indignation, as if he didn't even then elaborate on the fantasy, imagining where else he might pour that wine and drink it from.

"I can read your thoughts, remember," Oria said, giving him a pointed stare.

"*I* can read his thoughts and I'm no mind reader," Baeltya muttered back at her. They shared a smile and Lonen grinned without embarrassment.

Alby, Lonen's lieutenant on the battlefield and general assistant otherwise, who'd been discreetly lurking among the collection of attendants relieving them of their winter gear, stepped forward and bowed. "If I may, Your Highnesses, I can resolve this issue by informing you there will be a formal dinner this evening." He coughed into a fist rather than laugh at the dismay on Lonen's face. "To celebrate your return to health, to the throne, your engagement, etcetera."

"By whose command?" Lonen inquired politely enough,

though the growl in his voice belied it.

"Her Highness Queen Vycayla." Alby held his head high, but unfortunately ended the sentence on a bit of a squeak that made it sound rather like a question.

"I begin to understand why Nolan imprisoned our mother in her rooms," Lonen remarked thoughtfully, and Oria punched his arm.

"Lonen!"

He caught her fist easily in his big hand, moving faster than she could snatch it back. "Yes, my love—did you need something?"

She laughed, beyond relieved to see the merriment dancing in his gray eyes, the laugh lines crinkling around them. For a time, she'd worried that the trials, battles, and betrayals had killed his irreverent humor and sunny optimism. She should've known her barbarian would be more resilient than that.

"Go see your mother. And be polite," she said, tugging her hand free.

He sighed heavily. "Yes, dear."

She narrowed her eyes at him. "I don't have to marry you, remember. I can still—" She shrieked in laughing surprise as he caught her to him and kissed her breathless, uncaring of their considerable audience.

When he finally let her breathe, he cocked his crooked eyebrow at her, the scars—both old and new—making the gesture a bit twisted looking, and enticingly dangerous. "You were saying, my lady?"

"Nothing," she managed. She drew a deep breath and smiled at the wicked mischief on his face. "Nothing at all."

"Good." He set her on her feet. Seemed about to say something else… but shook his head like one of his wolfhounds shedding water. "Stay out of trouble, wife."

"Back at you, husband."

~ 3 ~

L ONEN ENDED UP escorting his mother into formal dinner. He hadn't seen Oria since they returned from flying. Alby had relayed a message via Baeltya that Oria would be occupying other rooms until the wedding, and that she'd dress there—wherever that was, as they all avoided saying exactly, determined to subvert their king's worst impulses by keeping the location a secret—and that Oria would meet him at dinner.

It hardly seemed fair, to be stuck with his sharp-tongued mother instead of his delectable wife, but the situation would be temporary. Very temporary, which had him in excellent spirits. He'd put his afternoon to good use, keeping himself too busy to obsess about bedding Oria. Much. Several dire matters required the king's attention, along with a great many only slightly less urgent ones.

He'd put Arnon in charge of designing a platform and new rooftop apartments, and his brother had leapt at the opportunity to take on the project, with almost embarrassing gratitude. No small part of it had to do with the enforced inactivity of winter, no doubt. But Arnon also seemed to feel he needed to make things right between them. Lonen had told him, in a private, intense conversation, that he understood Arnon's choices. He'd been torn between loyalties to his two elder brothers, one who should have been the rightful king, had fate played out as it should, and one who'd had kingship thrust upon him. Nolan had been convincing in his righteousness and paranoia. Had their positions been reversed, Lonen might have made the same choices Arnon did.

But Arnon didn't see it that way; instead questioning his own judgment and intelligence, because he hadn't realized Nolan wasn't himself. A difficult place for Arnon, who'd always been the cleverest, most learned, and most insightful of the four brothers.

"You gave Arnon a project, I hear," Vycayla commented as they strolled toward the great dining hall, as if she'd heard his thoughts. His mother was no sorceress, not like Oria, but she did have an uncanny knack for reading people.

"Yes. An engineering project that should absorb his energies until the weather thaws enough that we can get back to work restoring the aqueducts." He sounded slightly defensive.

"I'm not criticizing," she replied mildly. "It was kindly done, to give him an opportunity to do you a service, one that will benefit you and Oria personally."

"I don't need him to make anything up to me, I told him that."

"You might not need it, but he does. A wise ruler recognizes what his people need and gives them the opportunity to seize it, regardless of his own feelings."

Lonen snorted. "Never thought I'd see the day *you* called me wise."

"In point of fact, I didn't," she retorted in a tone tart enough to make him wince. "I was speaking hypothetically."

"Ah." He nodded to himself, assuming a sage expression rather than an aggravated rolling of his eyes at his mother. Eye rolling was probably not appropriate for a king, wise or not.

Vycayla stopped, turning to face him. They stood just shy

of the short corridor that opened into the main hall, out of earshot of the palace guards stationed there. "I do think you'll be a wise ruler, my son," she said, her gaze unusually soft with sentiment. "When you were a boy, even a very young man, I never thought you'd be the one to show the true mettle of your father and me. You've surprised me, happily so."

"Thank you, I think," he said, feeling his scar pull with the frown. His mother never did pay unadulterated compliments, so he should settle for that and be happy. Then, from the opposite direction, Oria stepped into the hall, Baeltya a step behind her, and all thoughts fled from his mind.

Vycayla turned at his expression and hummed in satisfaction. "Ah, Oria, you look lovely."

Oria smiled, pleased and also a bit abashed, her high cheekbones delicately flushed. They'd put her hair up in one of the elaborate piles of coils and braids the Destrye ladies of court favored, and it looked like a gorgeous crown of copper framing her piquant face. She wore a gown of light green, a sheer layer intricately beaded with copper swirls over a darker silk beneath—which wasn't that much less transparent. The fall of the gown outlined her slender limbs, her full breasts, narrow waist, and gave hints of the vee centered between the graceful arc of her slim hips. The sleeves parted at her shoulders, leaving her pale arms bare, and caught again at her wrists in copper-beaded cuffs. A slit in the narrow skirt of the gown showed flashes of her long legs as she walked toward him. Mouth-watering.

His mother cleared her throat. "Shall we step inside, Baeltya, and give them a moment?"

"Do you think it's safe, Your Highness?" Baeltya's voice rippled with suppressed laughter.

"He can hardly ravish her in the main hall," Vycayla replied dryly.

Lonen, who'd been fantasizing that very thing, quickly banished the image of Oria with her back against the nearby carved pillar, green skirts hiked around her waist and head thrown back in ecstasy as he plunged into her. Oria blushed a deeper pink, so he knew she'd seen it in his thoughts. He only grinned at her with wicked delight.

"You look beyond beautiful, love," he managed once Baeltya and Vycayla discreetly withdrew, and his voice came out rough. "The green suits you,"

"Thank you. It no longer seemed necessary to wear red, like a Báran priestess." She sounded almost shy as she looked down at herself, plucking at the gown self-consciously. "But I feel quite… naked."

Oh, if she only knew. "Are you cold?" he asked with hasty concern. His desert-bred bride had become more accustomed to the bitterness of Dru's winter, but she took chill easily.

Her mouth twisted in a wry smile, and she leaned closer, saying in a low, conspiratorial voice, "I'm using magic to keep myself warm. Is that wrong?"

Indeed, with her so close, he felt he'd entered a warm cloud of summer, with Oria its sun. The spicy perfume of the qinn that the Destrye ladies used wound together with Oria's natural scent, becoming somehow both uniquely her and redolent of home. "I'd like to strip you naked for real and lick every inch of you," he replied in a low growl of need. "Is that wrong?"

Her coppery eyes glittered with answering desire. "In the main hall of the palace, probably yes."

"It would make for good illustrations in the history books." He picked up her hand and kissed the silken back of it, then turned it over to press a passionate kiss to her palm, licking it in demonstration—and allowing the image of taking her, fast and hard against the nearby pillar, to bloom in his mind again.

She snatched her hand away, her breath lifting her breasts enticingly, her nipples hard against the clinging silk. "But perhaps not as we'd choose to be remembered," she noted breathlessly.

"Do any of us get to choose how we're remembered?" he countered, but he took up her hand and threaded it chastely through the crook of his elbow, turning to lead her into the hall for the feast. "I don't know, going down in Destrye history as a king and queen noted for their passionate love for each other would be a legacy I could happily embrace."

She slid him a sideways glance, one that he might've called demure for the way her long lashes veiled her gaze, except that her eyes glittered with wicked amusement. "As long as we're not the great cautionary tale used to teach Destrye children the folly of going to war against the walled cities of the desert, I'll be happy."

"There is that," he muttered agreement, pausing ceremoniously in the doorway so the assembly could rise and then bow to show honor.

"A nice change from the last formal dinner," Oria replied in the same quiet voice as she smiled radiantly for the court.

"Isn't it? It's much more pleasant to rule when people aren't looking for the first opportunity to put a blade in your back."

She muffled a laugh and he led her to the high table on the dais at one end of the room. The Haligne tree Oria had grown from a spoon as a demonstration of her magical skills at their last dinner party spread its limbs over the table, elaborate and sweetly blooming.

"Has that thing grown?" he whispered.

"I think so," she replied, equally hushed—and perhaps awed.

"How, without sunlight or soil?"

"I…don't know." She sounded a bit distressed, so he let it go. Arnon waited for them, standing next to his seat beside their two empty chairs at the center. He bowed again. "Your Highnesses."

"I'm not queen yet, Arnon," Oria replied, taking the hand he offered so she could sit.

"To me you are," he said with some fervency, looking to Lonen also. "Both of you, my king and queen, always."

Lonen gripped his shoulder. Then, on impulse, pulled him into a hug, pounding his back. As he did, he said into his brother's ear, "Relax. We're good."

Arnon returned the hug but shook his head slightly as he withdrew. "I have a lot to make up for."

On the other side of Oria, the dowager queen caught Lonen's eye, reminding him of their conversation with a significantly arched brow. "Fine, fine," he said. "Sit already." He raised his voice as he said it, giving permission to the assembly.

Salaya, his brother Ion's widow, standing by her chair at Vycayla's other hand, moved a bit more slowly than the rest, lingering to give him a nod. Her hair shorn short in mourning, Salaya's striking face stood in stark relief in the torchlight, her gaze speaking something. Then she looked away and sat.

They ate, the mood in the hall light, even festive. Oria received special plates of grains and vegetables, with cheese from the goats and buttered puff pastries, all prepared especially for her. Making happy noises, she ate heartily, the sight doing his heart good. Even his mother carried on pleasant conversations with Oria and Salaya, making an effort to be charming to her two daughters-in-law.

Arnon regaled Lonen with an impressive array of details on the planned addition to the palace, having accomplished a truly astonishing amount of work in the few hours since Lonen handed him the project. Listening—and nodding at hopefully appropriate intervals, since the in-depth explanation of stressors and load-bearing designs meant little to him—Lonen scanned the room, noting who was there and who wasn't.

"Sounds excellent," he said, when Arnon wound down. "As for your questions on the rooftop garden, ask Oria. She might be able to make some drawings for you."

"Oh, perfect." Arnon leaned around Lonen to smile at Oria, who nodded that she'd heard, though she listened to some tale of Vycayla's.

"I don't see Natly," Lonen said, as neutrally as possible, after what he hoped was a reasonable pause.

He didn't fool his brother, however, who gave him a sharp glance. "No. I didn't imagine you'd want to. Not after... last time."

When Natly, his former lover and would-be fiancée, had caused a scene—the one that led to Oria's display of sorcery. "I don't *want* to," he replied, maybe a bit too sharply. "But I've also learned to distrust who's out of sight, lest they be plotting something unpleasant."

That was the wrong thing to say, as Arnon's face creased unhappily, shadows of guilt and remorse darkening his eyes. "Natly is down with Nolan," he said before Lonen could take back the careless words or reassure his brother yet again that he harbored no suspicions or ill will. "I am having her watched. When Oria's not studying him, Natly slips down to the dungeon and sits with him."

"Interesting." And surprising. Though... was it? Nolan had

been the target of Natly's flirtations for quite some time before he brushed her off and she set her sights on Lonen, the next prince in line.

"I can put a stop to it," Arnon hastily assured him. "It seemed like a harmless occupation to me, and perhaps good for both of them."

"I have no problem with it." As he said it, he realized he felt quite the opposite. "Is he… rational, with her?"

Arnon shook his head. "Whatever happened, however your iron axe affected him, he hasn't put two rational words together since. And, to be frank, he was hardly better than that in your absence. From the moment he discovered you and Oria had fled in the night—" He cleared his throat, hesitating.

"Go ahead," Lonen urged him. "Speak freely."

Under the table, Oria put a hand on his knee, stroking softly. Not high enough to be titillating—or, rather, not distractingly so, since everything about her had his brain going in one direction—but a gesture of approval. In his peripheral vision, she seemed to be intently listening to Vycayla, but Oria possessed many skills, and had long since perfected the art of listening to several conversations at once—and probably to his thoughts, as well. Experimentally, he sent her a mental kiss, and she squeezed his knee in response. That answered that.

"He flew into such a rage," Arnon said quietly. "At first I agreed with him, that your abrupt escape signaled your guilt and, ahem, her influence over you. I'm sorry for that."

Lonen slipped his own hand under the table and took Oria's, lacing their fingers together, just for the pleasure of touching her. "You've apologized countless times already," Lonen said. "Let it go. I have."

Arnon set his jaw. "I'll decide when I can let this go. It took little time to see his madness—though longer for me to admit it. I was a fool."

Lonen moved Oria's hand up his thigh, noting the twitch of her full lips as she suppressed a smile. She didn't resist, squeezing the muscle a bit. "We are all fools at one time or another," Lonen said to Arnon. "What matters is you refused to support him when it mattered most."

"Seeing Mother here—discovering that she'd arrived and he'd had her arrested and imprisoned…" Arnon shook his head and shoved his plate away, as if the sight of it made him ill. "I have a great deal to make up to you both."

"Then do it," Lonen said, allowing a hint of impatience to creep into his voice. He tried to tug Oria's hand higher, but this time she did resist.

Arnon looked at him in shock, for his words and tone, Lonen realized—not his antics shrouded by the cloth on the table. "I need you," Lonen told his brother. "Even if Oria can cleanse the sorcery from Nolan's mind, I don't think I'll be able to trust him in the same way. You're the only brother I have left who I can rely on. Do what you need to in order to get your head on straight—but get it done. We have a lot to accomplish before the weather thaws and I'm going to be relying on you heavily. So…" He waved a hand in the air. "Get your own load-bearing supports shored up, or whatever."

Arnon's lips twitched, the shadows lightening. "I don't think that analogy plays very well."

"This is why I leave such things to you. I trust you to understand them."

Arnon sobered. "You really trust me—still? After everything?"

Lonen leveled his full attention on his brother, giving up the tussle under the table with Oria. "I trust you *more* than ever, after everything," he said with quiet emphasis. "We learn from our mistakes."

Arnon pressed his lips together, emotion shining bright in his eyes. "Thank you, Your Highness."

"All the times I pressed your face in the mud to get you to show your older brother some respect," Lonen said with a growl, "and *this* is what it takes."

Arnon snorted, sounding a bit more like his old, irreverent self. "You're much scarier now. And you have a super scary wife," he added, dragging his plate back and spearing a piece of meat.

Oria leaned over Lonen, eyes sparkling with mischief. "You have *no* idea, Arnon," and slid her hand up to squeeze Lonen's balls under the table.

A perfectly timed attack, as he'd been drinking a deep swallow of wine—so he choked on it, nearly spewing it across the table. He glared at Oria, who only laughed, a bell-like sound of complete delight.

"But not wife," she corrected, with an innocent smile for Lonen as she squeezed hard enough to make him wince. "Not until Arill says so. Only then will I have him to—"

"On that note," he interrupted, taking her hand off him and keeping it in a firm grip as he tugged her to her feet. "I have an announcement." The room quieted and Oria beamed up at him, mooning at him as if completely enraptured. Who knew that the minx would turn out to have such a mischievous sense of humor when she finally felt well? "The dowager Queen Vycayla, in her capacity as High Priestess of Arill, has determined the most auspicious date for the sorceress Oria, Princess of Bára, and I to wed."

Oria raised her brows at him for withholding that bit of information until now. He smiled at her easily, with lots of teeth, which he intended to use to torment her into shameless begging. The hall briefly buzzed with excitement, then fell quiet as everyone strained to hear.

"In Arill's Temple, as Sgatha rises full and Grienon briefly paces her tomorrow evening, Arill will set her hand as the final seal on our marriage, begun many months ago in Oria's City of Bára."

Everyone cheered, the hall in an uproar of toasts and celebratory shouts.

"Tomorrow night?" Oria practically squeaked, not only because of his arm tight around her. "I didn't expect it so soon!"

He looked down into her upturned face, her copper eyes glinting with gold in the torchlight. "Last chance for second thoughts," he said quietly, cursing himself for a fool even as he said it. As if he'd be able to let her go. No. No, if she wanted out, he would let her go. He would be a better man, a better king than his barbarian ancestors.

"You're truly asking me that, Lonen?" Oria breathed, a straight light in her face.

"Yes," he answered gravely, his heart stuttering to a stop. "I'm asking you to marry me, Oria. And if the answer is no, I'll respect that."

"Hmm…" She looked thoughtful, then burst out laughing. Reaching up, she wound her fingers in his hair, which he'd left loose because she liked it that way. Tugging his head down, she kissed him. "If you tried to get away," she said against his lips, "I'd toss you over Buttercup's back and keep you captive in the hills until you broke down and agreed to marry me. Again."

Deep inside, where the marriage bond connected to his heart and soul, heat and joy burned like the sun over Bára.

~ 4 ~

ORIA HAD THOUGHT that the temporary set of rooms they'd given her were far too spacious and extravagant, especially for one person, for a few short days. Now it seemed Vycayla had been prescient in suggesting Oria move into the suite the queen had lived in before she left Dru, because the considerable space teemed with women, most sewing or crafting something, all of them talking at high volume.

Oria thanked Arill or whoever might be listening that she'd learned to shield effectively. There was a time this kind of crowd—and excited emotional energy—would've had her fainting within minutes. They'd swarmed her rooms at dawn with fabric, patterns, jewelry, and keen urgency just shy of panic. Barely an hour later, Oria had taken refuge in a large, thronelike chair that served to give her an island of space in the sea of giggling and chattering women, sipping the hot tea she finally had a moment to drink inside the dubious barricade of the heavy, ornate arms.

"I could breathe some flame and chase them all away," Chuffta offered, making her smile.

"Thank you, but I'm fine. At least they're all here to bring off the wedding in fine form. I'm grateful for the help."

"Oria." Vycayla approached her chair with a determined lift to her chin, a swath of green silk the color of moss draped over her arms. "We should make your wedding dress from this. It's the best choice. Once you agree, the seamstresses can start cutting."

They'd already taken her measurements—every part of her—in a dizzyingly fast examination. She'd been relieved to put on her dressing robe and escape their discussion of her body's finest qualities, and what would be best concealed. The Destrye women were honest and frank in a way that Báran women were decidedly not. Only the knowledge that they didn't mean to embarrass her, or insult her in any way, had salved her raw reactions. At least Lonen loved her body as it was.

"So do I," Chuffta pointed out.

"Yes, but you don't count."

"Hey!"

"Oria." Vycayla snapped impatient fingers. "All I need is a yes."

"It's very pretty," Oria offered. Behind Vycayla, Baeltya shook her head emphatically. "But…"

"But?" Vycayla demanded.

Oria looked to Baeltya for clues—and rescue.

"I thought you might prefer this red," Baeltya said smoothly, drawing up a young Destrye girl who nearly drowned in a pile of crimson velvet. "As is traditional for your people," Baeltya added, with a glance at Vycayla.

"Oria will be married in Arill's Temple via her holiest rites," Vycayla argued. "She should wear Arill's colors."

"If I may," Oria began, but both women ignored her.

"Oria is not a priestess of Arill," Baeltya countered. "And this wedding is a joining of Bára and Dru. Dress the king in Arill's colors and Oria in Báran ones."

"Oria may not be a priestess of Arill, *yet*," Vycayla countered, "but once she marries my son and is acknowledged Queen of the Destrye, then she will be expected to take up the mantle of serving Arill, which means she should begin as she means to go on, wearing Arill's colors." With a triumphant huff, she held out the fabric to Oria. "Yes."

Not a question at all, and Oria opened her mouth, hoping words would come to explain how she felt. A somewhat desperate hope, as she had trouble defining to herself what those feelings were.

"You don't have to capitulate to her, Oria," Baeltya inserted, eyes flashing and dark curls tumbling as she shook her hair back behind her shoulders, thrusting forward the crimson cloth. "This is *your* wedding and you should be able to come to it as the person you are. Who you decide to be after this is your decision."

"I think—" Oria started to say.

"Nonsense." Vycayla leveled a fierce gray glare on the shorter healer, reminding Oria very much of Lonen in battle mode. "No queen—or princess—is wholly her own person. Oria never has been and she won't be going forward. The Queen of Dru is *always* also the head healer and priestess of Arill." Vycayla emphasized her words with the green silk.

"Oria's magic isn't healing. She's a powerful sorceress with skills not seen in Dru for centuries. She will carve her own path." Baeltya shook the crimson velvet.

"Ladies, I—" Once again, Oria got no further. With a sigh, she set her teacup down.

"Exactly," Vycayla crowed in triumph. "Centuries of *tradition*. Therefore, she—"

Oria sent a chilling gust of wind through the room and stood, letting the power glow from her. She might look silly, bundled into her dressing robe and warm socks, with her hair still a tumbled mess from sleep, but the room went silent, all the busy women stilled at their tasks, gaping at her.

"Your Highness," she said, not unkindly, inclining her head and smiling. "Healer Baeltya. I greatly appreciate your efforts to make this wedding truly spectacular, and I know Lonen does, too." A blatant lie there as Lonen felt no such thing. As they parted after the feast the night before, he'd sent her an array of images of what he'd rather be doing than sleeping alone and muttered dire threats about his mother in Oria's ear before Baeltya firmly tugged her away. It made a laugh rise in her heart to think of it, which only added to the warmth of her smile. "The sorcerers of my people make these decisions based on certain arcane messages," she continued, embroidering on the lie shamelessly. "Perhaps if I could see the fabric choices, then the magic will indicate the most serendipitous choice for this most blessed ritual."

Vycayla studied her with a shrewd gaze, not really taken in by Oria's story, but also unwilling to call her a liar in front of so many people. Baeltya suppressed a grin, turning it into a solemn nod. "Of course, Sorceress Oria. If you'll step into the anteroom with me?"

Oria nearly gasped aloud at the sight that greeted her in the next room. The spacious receiving room was positively stuffed with fabrics of all colors and textures. None of the heavy wooden furniture showed, as every surface had been draped with fabric.

"Overwhelming, I know," Vycayla commented dryly from behind her. "Thus I thought to spare you."

Oria gave her a radiant smile, mostly faked. It was that or say something unforgivable. "I dare say as Queen of Dru I'll have to make more difficult decisions than this. I am beyond impressed to see such an array of fabrics," she added to salve

Vycayla's irritation. "Are these all created by the Destrye?"

"No." Vycayla softened, and Baeltya tossed Oria an amused smile behind the dowager queen's back as the tall, imposing woman moved into the room, her long fingers testing the various fabrics with tenderness. She'd braided her floor-length hair and left it in a tail down the middle of her back. Even braided, the tip of her hair brushed the hem of her skirts. "The Destrye enjoyed vibrant trade with the lands to the south back in the day."

Back before the Báran golems came, she meant. Before Oria's people drained the lakes of Dru and drove the Destrye nearly to destruction.

"The queen before me and the queen before her collected many of these, and as a young queen I continued in the same vein, seeking out the most beautiful fabrics from every ship and merchant train. They've been stored in chests of wood that banish insects, preserved all this time." She sighed, no longer vibrating with ruthless determination, and waved a hand. "Choose whichever you like, Oria. It's time we had a queen again who looks the part."

Oria hesitated, taking in the severe dowager queen, hair pulled back tightly from her face in that braid, her gown one she must have brought from the hermitage, an undyed woven cloth no doubt spun from crops they'd grown. "There are more seamstresses here than can possibly all work on one gown at the same time, Your Highness," she said softly. "Perhaps the green silk should be made into one for you."

Vycayla looked surprised, glancing at the lengths of shimmering green she'd set aside, her fingers going to it and stroking with that same tenderness. "We'll see," she murmured. Then her gray gaze flashed to Oria's with granite command. "Now choose. We can't spend all morning dithering over this one decision."

Not when they had countless decisions to dither over for the rest of the day, Oria thought to herself, but circumspectly did not say aloud.

"This is why derkesthai don't wear clothes," Chuffta said cheerfully, if a bit snidely. *"So much time wasted on colors. Be the color you are naturally."*

"I think even the Destrye would be shocked if I arrived at my wedding ceremony naked." Oria wandered through the maze of fabrics, her eye unable to settle on one.

"Lonen likes you naked. He—"

"Stop! Don't go there."

Chuffta snickered in her mind, well-pleased with himself. And her eye landed on a length of shimmering copper silk. *"Ooh,"* Chuffta crooned. *"See? That one matches your coloring. Do that one."*

She had to agree, picking up the fragile silk and stroking it, realizing as she did that she touched it with the same affectionate tenderness Vycayla had shown for the green silk. It was so sheer and smooth that it snagged infinitesimally on the skin of her fingers, though Oria would've sworn they were soft and free of blemishes. Metallic threads ran through the copper-dyed silk, giving the overall fabric a magical sparkle.

"That one has been in the stores for as long as anyone can remember," Vycayla said quietly, reaching out to touch it also. "It was old when I was a little girl."

Oria reluctantly let it go. "I'll pick something else."

Vycayla raised her brows in an amused arch. "And save it for what? Perhaps our predecessor was guided by Arill to purchase the fabric for you, for when you came along." She gestured to a patiently waiting seamstress. "This one."

"It really is perfect for you, Oria," Baeltya said with a genuine smile of pleasure. "It could indeed have been chosen by the goddess for you."

"It seems to me that you all invoke Arill to support whatever outcome you'd like to see," Oria muttered before she thought about how it would sound. "I mean—"

But Vycayla laughed, and Baeltya grinned broadly. Vycayla put her hands on Oria's shoulders and steered her back to the living area being used as the workroom. "Now you're learning. I think you'll do just fine as Queen of Dru."

A surprising flush of pleasure suffused her to have the good opinion of Lonen's mother. Not many people in Oria's life had expressed such confidence in her.

"*I think you'll do very well, too,*" Chuffta said, his mind-voice ever so slightly indignant.

"*You don't count,*" she reminded him with a mental laugh.

"*Hey!*"

"*Because you love me and think I'm wonderful no matter what I do.*"

"*Oh. Well that's true.*"

LONEN ADJUSTED THE fit of his formal clothes. His tailor sprang forward with a chiding click of his teeth to put it back again. "It should hang thus, Your Highness," he said, the deferential tone changing nothing.

Sitting nearby with a mug of ale, Arnon smiled, tight-lipped, suppressing his laughter. Lonen gave him a dark look. "Laugh all you like, brother. You get to wear your usual clothing."

"True," Arnon agreed cheerfully enough, "but then, I have decent clothing to wear. How did you end up entirely with fighting leathers and hunting gear?"

"I've been busy," Lonen muttered.

"Still, I would've thought that Natly, at least… Ah." Arnon hit the realization and closed his mouth over it.

"Yes," Lonen said, holding still as his man produced a cloak of deep forest green and fastened it around Lonen's shoulders with a hammered metal clasp in the shape of a stylized tree. "I didn't want to marry Oria wearing clothes chosen by another woman."

"Good thinking," Arnon murmured. "And the green is a good choice. Honoring Arill. Peace and fertility, rather than war."

Looser fitting that what he normally wore, the silk trousers and shirt fell in crisp lines, in a green so dark it looked black until the light hit it just right. A thick leather belt decorated with hammered metal leaves cinched the shirt at his waist, and the sleeves billowed with so much extra fabric it would hamper him in a fight.

But, as his tailor had retorted when he pointed that out, today was not for fighting. It gave Lonen pause to realize how much anticipating conflict, the daily battles, had become ingrained in his thinking. One day he'd like to be a king who expected every day to be peaceful.

A nice dream, anyway.

"Is everything ready?" he asked Arnon.

"Yes." Arnon set the mug down and stood. "A temporary solution, but the structure should hold for the short time we need it. It will be a good test case for the long-term stress and stability of the final design."

Lonen paused, running those words back through his head.

"Is that code for 'it could come down at any time?'"

"Oh no." Arnon shook his head emphatically. "It's code for 'it could come down eventually, but not today.' Which isn't a concern, because we'll dismantle the platform after the ceremony and reuse everything for the permanent structure."

"Hmm." Lonen eyed his man as he approached with the wreath of Dru, his crown, now shining and cleaned of his brother's blood, at least physically.

"You said you trusted me," Arnon said, a hint of doubt creeping into his voice.

"What? No, not that. I absolutely trust that you wouldn't want me crushed by logs on my wedding day. It's that." He waved a hand at the wreath and sighed, his man hesitating in trepidation.

"It's yours by right, and by Arill's clear decision," Arnon said quietly.

"I keep seeing it covered in Nolan's blood," he told Arnon, trusting him with that, too. "I can't get that image of my mind."

Arnon cocked his head thoughtfully. "He wore a crown he stole to a duel. It's not a metaphor, not an omen. Anything you wear to a duel is going to get blood on it. That's just biology."

Lonen blinked at his brother. "That's a remarkably practical approach."

Arnon shrugged cheerfully. "I've always been the practical one." He took the wreath from Lonen's man with a nod and settled it on Lonen's head himself. "Wear it with pride and no remorse, brother," he said. "Arill knows I'm glad it's not mine."

Together they strode out, climbing the stairs to the upper levels of the palace, bypassing the Bridge of Seofe that led to Arill's Temple. Arnon had performed miracles, recruiting an army of otherwise bored and idle Destyre warriors to construct a flat platform atop the pitched roof. They had to climb a ladder for the last level up, but Arnon had at least designed it to rest at a long angle with broad, flat steps, so hopefully Oria wouldn't have trouble navigating it. Other ladies, arriving in their finery for the royal wedding, seeming to be having no trouble.

Atop the platform, hammered metal basins all along the edges held blazing fires which helped dispel the wintery chill as the sun declined to the horizon and the dusky purple evening descended. Arill's tree showed raw cuts where nearby branches had been severed, and the smell of fresh sap filled the crisp air, along with the sweet smoke of the fires. A bower of evergreen bows had been constructed at one end, between sunset and moonrise, and Rhiten Robson waited there in his formal priest's robes the color of new leaves in spring, lavishly embroidered in gold.

Lonen slipped his hand into his pocket, checking that the ring remained safely within, beyond glad that he'd commissioned the metalsmith to begin work on it before he and Oria fled the palace.

"Nervous?" Arnon asked as they bided their time, waiting for the bride and her retinue. The priest kept an eye on the sky, keenly observant of the timing, but Lonen knew his mother wouldn't let Oria be late, even if she had to drag his Báran bride there naked.

"Eager," Lonen replied with a wolfish smile, making his brother laugh. "Recall that Oria and I have been married some months now. This is a formality for me."

"True." Arnon regarded him speculatively. "Were you nervous then? Marrying a foreign sorceress in some arcane ritual of the bloodthirsty Báran people and all?"

"Terrified," Lonen confessed in a wry tone. He met his brother's amused gaze. "I would have given a great deal to have you with me then. I'm grateful to have you with me now."

Amusement fled, gripped by emotion, Arnon clasped his shoulder. "Now and always," he replied in a rough voice. The drums started up and Arnon glanced to the side, eyes widening. He whistled low and soft. "And look how well all of this has turned out for you."

Lonen turned to see Oria rising with measured steps up the long ladder, Baeltya and his mother on either side of her. The last rays of the sun caressed her with loving fingers, stoking the fire in her hair, which fell in a blazing sheet like molten metal, over a gown the same color. Suspended by chains of copper inset with jewels, the fine fabric barely clung to her breasts before falling in a shimmering drape of sparkling light. The same sort of chain draped around her pale throat, holding on a cloak of emerald green lined with more of the copper silk. A gold band crossed her forehead, holding the veil of hair off her lovely, fine-boned face. She smiled at him, her lips painted the glossy shade of good wine, and her eyes shone brighter than any of the jewels she wore.

He held out a hand to her and she took it, looking him up and down. "Who knew my barbarian warrior would clean up so well?" she murmured. "You'd put even a peacock of a Báran nobleman to shame."

"Oh, I'm still a barbarian brute under these pretty clothes," he replied in the same tone. "As I plan to demonstrate with great vigor very soon."

A high flush graced her cheekbones. "I look forward to that demonstration, my king."

"Excellent news, my queen. Are you ready to marry me

again?"

"Again and again," she replied with a radiant smile, that only briefly dimmed. "I only wish Chuffta could be here, more than mentally."

"He can and will. Call him."

Oria frowned. "What do you mean?"

Lonen pointed to the cleared area beyond Arnon, who grinned at her in great excitement, practically hopping from foot to foot. "My wedding gift to you both," Arnon said.

Oria's welled with tears, though her joyful smile never dimmed. "Thank you," she whispered, seeming too overcome to speak more loudly.

Moments later, a white shadow passed overhead, the wind of Chuffta's wings making the bonfires flare. Lonen kept half an eye on them, but the drafts quickly waned.

"I'm telling him to be his very most careful," Oria murmured. Sure enough, Chuffta soon settled on the nearby platform in a roped-off space kept clear for him. The wooden platform groaned ominously—and Arnon frowned, scanning the area, clearly taking mental notes—but it held. Chuffta folded his wings and curved his neck, lowering his triangular head to rest his pointed chin on the platform, for all the world like a cat settling in to rest.

Rhiten Robson cleared his throat and they turned to him. Holding out his arms, he pointed one finger to the setting sun, and the other toward the opposite horizon, where Sgatha's curve emerged, round and the color of a rose from Oria's garden. Like a blue-green jewel, Grienon rose beside her. They'd cleared branches to make the sight visible, Lonen realized, and a breath of awe sighed through the gathering.

A sacred moment, indeed, full of the peace he and Oria would bring to the world.

~ **5** ~

MONTHS AND FOREVER ago, Lonen had promised he'd show Oria how the Destrye did a wedding. He'd grumbled at the lack of celebration at their Báran one—though having the bride collapse unconscious hadn't helped what was admittedly an intense and solemn ritual.

This was the party Lonen had promised back then, when she'd been so uncertain of what the future held. That uncertainty lingered—they had a war still to fight—but for this one night, they could revel in the best sense of the word. Music played, the hides stretched across the hammered metal drums sending a booming beat through the forest, while pipes carved of wood and fashioned of metal wove higher and mellower melodies around the throbbing rhythm. The fires blazed, sending sparks up into the sky, and Lonen guided her through the unfamiliar dance steps, grinning in delight as she held onto him and followed along.

The dances weren't difficult, but they often involved him bodily lifting her to swing her in a circle, making her shriek with surprise and laughter. The Destrye woman did likewise as their partners swung them in wild patterns, making her less self-conscious, the female voices rising high as the men shouted in counterpoint, stomping their feet—a human version of the song made by the pipes and drums.

Arnon's platform shuddered beneath their feet—and once she spotted him lying on his belly, head hanging over the edge as he checked a support—but it held. To be on the safe side, she sent Chuffta off again, and he went easily, wishing her a happy night with her mate, and anticipating a nice bloody cow from the Destrye herds a short distance away.

She was just as happy not to be in on that hunt.

Lonen lifted her higher and she clutched his shoulders, sending up a whoop with the other women as she nearly flew, the copper and gold ring on her finger glinting against the black-emerald silk of his fine shirt. Lonen's teeth flashed white in his black beard, trimmed close and neat for the occasion, the hammered gold leaves in the wreath nestled in his black curls glinting. Her barbarian king.

The music finished in a triumphant crash, but Lonen didn't set her down. Instead he slipped an arm under her knees, cradling her against his muscular chest. "Have you danced enough?" he asked, a wicked sparkle in his eyes.

She wound her hands behind his neck, under the hair so tidily tied back, ready to see it falling around his face. "Why— do you have a better offer?"

"I'm thinking a more private celebration is in order. If you've enjoyed the party enough. I don't want you to miss the fun."

"I think there will be other celebrations, yes?" she breathed, desire and anticipation flaring as hot and bright in her body as the bonfires. "Other times to dance."

"We'll dance every night, if you like," he said, and she knew he'd follow through on that promise, as he had on every other.

"Then let's go," she said with a smile, caressing the back of his neck. "If it's polite to—"

"I am taking my wife to bed!" Lonen roared, and the gathering of Destrye shouted their approval.

Oria dissolved into embarrassed giggles, covering her hot face as Lonen carried her through the gathering, people calling out astonishingly ribald suggestions. "That answers that," she said, laughing.

"We *are* barbarians," Lonen noted with a toothy smile, agilely descending the half-ladder/half-staircase she'd so painstakingly climbed. "What did you expect when you wedded one?"

She levered herself up, threading her fingers through his thick curls, now coming loose around his face from the vigorous movements of the wild dancing, and kissed him with all the hunger in her. He growled deep in his throat, returning and deepening the kiss. Tugging loose the tie that bound his hair, Oria recognized the feel of it. Bemused, she studied it when Lonen broke the kiss to hasten his stride. The tie was a simple leather one, nothing as fancy as the rest of his garb. It was the one he'd accidentally left behind in Bára when he returned home with his Destrye armies, when she thought she'd never see him again.

She'd kept it, a girlish memento of the exuberantly masculine barbarian warrior who'd so stunned her senses and awakened in her such darkly sexual feelings. When he'd returned—to angrily accuse her of breaking their tentative peace, an argument that ended in her proposing a marriage of state—she'd given the leather tie back to him. And he'd worn the stained old thing to their wedding.

He saw her studying it. "It seemed right to wear it today. When I saw you kept that tie, that's when I knew."

"Knew what?" She arched a cool brow, but her heart swelled tight in her breast.

"That you wanted me," he murmured, a sensual rumble that crawled down her spine to her groin.

"I did not," she replied with indignation.

"You thought about me, fantasized about me."

"I didn't even realize I had it." She added a lofty sniff for good measure, which became a gasp when he took her earlobe in his teeth and nipped, then laved his hot tongue over the sting.

"You had it on the table beside your favorite seat in the garden. I imagine you sat there in your tower and looked out over the deserts toward Dru, imagining what I might be doing."

"I never—"

"You know how I know this?" He moved through the doors the guards opened. Vaguely Oria recognized the rooms as Vycayla's suite, rather than Lonen's old, smaller one. "I know because I was doing the same thing," Lonen continued before she could say anything about the rooms. He set her on her feet and unhooked the chain holding on her cloak, letting it fall to the floor. "I dreamed of you every night, and I'd wake longing for you. I'd look toward Bára, at Sgatha's rosy face and Grienon's fleeting passage, and envy the moons because they could look on you when I couldn't."

"Lonen…" she breathed, uncertain what words could follow that.

He framed her face in his big, rough hands and kissed her with infinite tenderness. "I love you, Oria. I think I loved you the moment I saw you in that window, as if lit from within by magic. You made me believe in the possibility of beauty, of peace and happiness, just by existing."

"I think it was slower for me," she answered with painful honesty, winding the tie between her fingers. "You frightened me so."

Quick concern creased his face. "Do I frighten you still?"

She laughed, letting her magic swell between them, caressing him with it so his eyes flared from granite to silvery gray. "Not in the least. That was more about me, and my own fears and insecurities. I was such a timid mouse."

"No." He brushed his thumbs over her cheekbones. "Never that. I thought you were the bravest person I'd ever beheld, riding out to surrender the city—and make demands of your conqueror."

She made a dismissive sound. "Nonsense, barbarian. You will never conquer me."

"Good." He took her hand and led her into the next room. All the wedding preparation detritus had disappeared, replaced with white candles and bows of evergreen. Bowls of hammered metal caught the candlelight and overflowed with autumn leaves, carefully dried to preserve their vibrant, fiery colors. "A Destrye tradition," he said, gazing around the room with her. "Evergreen for winter, autumn leaves, candles for the summer sun. Unfortunately we have no flowers for spring, but soon enough I'll be able to offer you real ones."

Oria summoned a bit of magic, remembering the pool at the edge of the forest where she and Lonen had rested and he'd told her they were in Dru. Touching one of the boughs of evergreen, she transformed it into a garland of yellow flowers, sweetly scented and with buttery petals.

"Buttercups," Lonen said, a hint of awe in his voice. "Fitting."

"Yes." She returned his smile. "Now we have everything."

"Almost." He pulled her into his arms, lips brushing hers, rapidly becoming a fire that consumed her. "I wanted this first time to be slow, romantic," he muttered against her mouth.

"but I don't know if I can be that restrained. Oria…" He groaned her name, his mouth slanting over her throat, kissing, licking, lightly biting here and there, and she went boneless.

"Where's a pillar when you need one?" she returned and he laughed, hoarse and desperate.

"Take off this gorgeous gown or I'll ruin it."

"I don't care." She arched in his grip, happy to have him tear the fragile cloth from her if it got him inside her faster.

"Oh no." He set her away from him and backed up to sit on the high bed, one hand gripping the other, a determined set to his jaw. "You'll wear that dress every year on the anniversary of our wedding, so I can remember this night."

"You might forget otherwise?" she teased, holding up her hair to reach behind her shoulders to unfasten the braided chain straps.

"Never," he averred, gaze intent on her. She swayed a little in place, enjoying his eyes on her.

"What if I get fat? Maybe I won't be able to fit into the dress after I've birthed ten children." She had the chains unhooked but held the copper silk coyly to her breasts.

"Is that how many you plan to have?" He quirked the scarred brow.

"At least. Maybe twice that many."

"Then I'll find more of that cloth and we'll keep adding to it, even if you're as big as Chuffta."

She laughed, delighted with him. Then let the silk fall, pooling at her feet. She wore nothing beneath—any undergarments would have showed through the delicate fabric—so she stood naked but for the simple slippers and the cloak of her hair. The ladies had wanted to put her hair up, but she'd insisted on having it down, knowing how Lonen loved it that way—and only finally agreed to the circlet as a sign of her station. Now she tugged it from her hair, tossed it aside, kicked off the slippers and moved to her husband, fully naked.

His eyes roved over her with a hunger she hoped he'd never lose. In his eyes, she wasn't too thin, and she believed she'd never be too fat. In his eyes she saw the same love she felt, the deep connection throbbing along the bond created long before the Báran priestesses solidified it with magic. A bond they created between them, despite their warring nations and the storied hatreds they'd been taught.

Lonen's eyes rose to her face with wry humor, as if he sensed her thoughts, and she opened her mind more fully to him, seeing herself as he did. "I think one of us is wearing too many clothes," she murmured.

HE LET OUT a shaking laugh and stood. "You blind me, Oria. I lose all sense around you."

"Then let me help," she answered in that smooth murmur, her nimble fingers moving to undo the clasp holding on his cloak, then the belt. She smoothed her hands over his chest as she parted his shirt, leaning in to press her soft lips to his skin—which might as well have been a brand, the way the touched seared through him. He fisted his hands by his sides, trying to control the nearly violent need to seize her and thrust himself inside her sweet body.

"Oria." He marveled at how calm he sounded. "If I promise you can play with me all you like later, would you get on the bed already and spread your pretty thighs for me?"

Her startled gaze flew up to his, the copper hot as melted

ore. She pursed her lips thoughtfully and he seriously considered kissing her senseless. "If you promise…" Turning, she climbed onto the bed, pausing on hands and knees to look over her shoulder, the gleaming fall of her hair sliding over her white skin, her gorgeous ass in the air and shapely legs parted to reveal her copper nether curls and the sweet pink flesh between. "But you're still wearing too many clothes," she purred.

He was, as the near-painful press of his engorged cock against the trousers attested. And he'd thought they were loose. Kicking off his boots, he stripped off the pants and crawled onto the bed after her, feeling much like an adolescent boy again, drooling after his first woman. With a mischievous smile, Oria—now leaning back on her elbows, giving him an excellent view of her delectable, pink-tipped breasts—scooted back across the big bed, daring him to come after her.

With an impatient snarl, he snagged one slim ankle, dragging her toward him, and she shrieked with surprise and laughter. Grabbing the other ankle before she could kick at him, he spread her wide and crawled up between her spread thighs, positioning himself at her entrance. Abruptly and completely serious, she gazed up at him, winding her arms behind his neck, lips parted and eyes full of emotion. He lowered himself, sliding his body against hers, savoring the connection of skin against skin, hers softer than the finest cloth. "Hold onto me," he murmured.

"Until the end of time," she replied.

He kissed her, savoring the way she arched into him, her little nipples hard against his chest, and he slipped a hand between them, her hot sex slick and ready, to his immense relief. Making another promise, this one to himself, that he could play with her later, too, he moved his hand under her slim hips, adjusting the angle and pressing his cock slowly into her.

Pulling back, he watched her face, the heavy-lidded look of concentration in her eyes as she felt his flesh enter hers. She was no virgin, not after the many games they'd played—and various implements he'd used on her—but she also had never had a man inside her. It had to be different, especially as he'd been too desperate to have her to bring her to climax a few times before this moment.

She moaned, long and low—and he stilled, worried that had been a mistake and he was hurting her. His arms shook with the effort at restraint, but he made himself wait until her eyes opened more fully, looking at him in wonder. "Don't stop," she breathed. "You feel so good."

With a gusty exhale, he let himself go, sliding into her tight sheath to the hilt until she surrounded him. Her breath hitched and she ground herself against him where their bodies joined, her skin growing slick against his. He dropped his forehead to hers, taking a shuddering breath, willing himself not to come immediately—incredibly difficult with her internal muscles gripping him like a hand.

"Lonen." She said his name like a plea, like a prayer. "Oh, my love. Please."

Unleashed, he moved, sliding out and in again. She bowed against him with a cry, her body a taut arch, thrumming like a bowstring, nails scoring down his back. He pulled back as much as he could bear—and home again, no longer able to be gentle, holding her hips in place as he plundered her sweet body, drinking in her cries of wild pleasure, her magic sparking all along his skin, enveloping him as he fell into her.

Oblivion, black and sprinkled with bright stars, claimed him. With something between a groan and a shout, he spent himself inside of her.

Dragging himself out of the depths, he managed to roll onto his side, loving her sound of protest as he withdrew from her. She followed along, rolling onto one hip and snuggling against him, pressing herself against his skin at every point of contact possible.

"I dreamed of this," she murmured, lips brushing his chest as she said it, a spoken kiss of movement. "Being this close to another person, touching like this—and my dreams never came close to this... *feeling*. I never knew it could be so mesmerizing, delightful, and somehow nurturing."

He knew what she meant. It felt as if she entered his very pores, assuaging a thirst he hadn't realized plagued him until it was slaked. "Any person at all?" he teased.

She laughed softly, a huff of air against his skin that had his groin tightening again, but in a lazy, sated ripple. He could have her as often as he liked, hold her just like this, for always. The knowledge settled something in him, made the trials ahead seem of little consequence, if he could always return to this.

He felt her shift, tipping her head back to look at him, so he opened his eyes. She looked sleepy, equally sated, almost feline in her smug contentment. "For a long time, I thought it would be my ideal mate, you know—the mysterious priest who would be the perfect match, his grien to my sgath—and I imagined this glorious harmony, where we'd feel like one person, where I'd no longer know where I left off and he began."

Lonen ignored the prickle of inadequacy. He'd long ago accepted that he could never be the perfect, harmonious match Oria had expected as part of her sorcerous birthright.

"And now," she continued, threading her fingers through

his chest hair, trailing her nails lightly over his skin, "I recognize how meaningless that was. How utterly foolish of me to want that."

"What do you mean?" he asked carefully, the surge of hope proving how little he'd actually ignored that jealous prickle.

She gave him a very serious look. "The keenest joy is finding connection in someone *unlike* me. When I was in the cavern with the derkesthai king, he told me I had to find the balance between extremes, that the purest magic resides in balance of both. In Bára, they always said it was a balance of sgath and grien, but I think they lost the truth of it somewhere along the way. I think it's this." She tugged his chest hair with a mischievous smile. "You and me, opposites, with a seed of each in the other."

He caressed her cheek, brushing the shining hair back from her high forehead. "We make a good team. I never expected to marry a woman like you."

"No." Her smile widened wickedly. "*You* were going to marry Natly!" She dug her nails painfully into his chest, making him yelp and clap a hand over hers.

"Never," he protested, rolling her onto her back and pinning her. "She was like your fantasy perfect husband—a distraction to pass the time until I found the real thing."

"Truly?" She breathed the question, searching his face, and it occurred to him that he might not be the only one vulnerable to that prick of uncertainty.

"Look into my heart and mind and you'll know," he assured her, brushing a kiss against that tempting mouth, savoring the taste of her.

She opened to him, as if she, too, wanted to drink him in. His cock grew against her soft thigh and she chuckled. "Again—already?"

"And again and again and again," he replied as he, unable to resist that lure of being surrounded by her, slid into her body, her sigh of pleasure like a song.

She wrapped her legs around his hips, trailing gentle caresses over him. "And again," she whispered. "And always."

~ **6** ~

WHEN THE LAST deep ripples of pleasure faded, Lonen rolled onto his side again, murmuring an apology for crushing her. Oria hadn't minded though. She'd loved feeling him lose himself in her, his mind going thoughtless but for the sensations of her, his love and delight in her bathing every pore like soaking in a perfumed and steaming bath. She whimpered a little as he slid out of her, leaving her empty again.

"Are you sore?" he asked, levering up on an elbow, a concerned frown twisting his scarred eyebrow, the flickering candlelight softening his features.

"No," she answered honestly, throwing her arms over her head and stretching in luxurious satiety. "I just miss having you inside of me."

He smiled, a hint of surprise coming from him and he stroked a big hand over her body, lingering to cup her breast, tracing the curve of her waist to her hip and down her thigh, his gaze following the movement. Feeling like a cat being petted, she wished she could purr. "I like being inside you," he said, gaze returning to hers, eyes full of silvery heat. "But I promised you other pleasures, too."

"We've done those," she replied. "I like those things, but this is new."

He laughed, levering himself up and going for a basin of

water set over a warming candle on a nearby table. Sweet herbs and dried flower petals floated in the water and when he handed her a cloth soaked in it, the steamy fragrance rose up. She cleaned herself, moving leisurely to draw his eye. He stood by the bed, cleaning himself also, his heavy cock now lax. Wicked desire shimmered from him, his thoughts shuttered, and she wondered what he might be planning.

"Believe me, what I have in mind is new also." He held out a hand for her cloth and she gave it to him with a little pout— one difficult to maintain at the sight of his gorgeous behind flexing as he returned the bowl and floating cloths to the warmer. She'd seen him naked plenty of times, but it seemed she'd never get enough.

He joined her on the bed again, tossing back the furs to expose her fully. Pleased with his admiration, she slid her legs together, a sinuous dance for him alone.

"You are so beautiful, Oria," he said throatily, crawling over to straddle her on his hands and knees, "and I plan to taste every bit of your luscious body."

Languidly she slid her arms around his neck, ready to draw him into a deep kiss. And he obliged her, but only with a brush of lips. Instead of sinking onto her, he moved to brush soft kisses along her jaw, to the sweet spot under her ear that made her shiver, then down her throat. She moaned, low and long, a sort of human purr, and he made an answering hum of pleasure.

Her arms fell back heavy as he continued to explore, lingering over the thin-skinned pulse points and slight hollows that sent her senses thrumming. Sometimes he nipped lightly, other times bestowed soft rains of fluttering kisses, followed by hot licks, then drawing her skin into his mouth as if he would devour her in truth.

She dissolved into a flurry of soft cries and pleas. Plucking at his shoulders, she tried to urge him between her spread thighs, but he wouldn't be moved, instead taking her hand in his to deeply kiss her palm, then each fingertip, drawing her fingers one by one into his mouth, an indescribable sensual delight. He kissed his way down her arm, lingering at the hollow of her elbow, then tracing the tender underside of her arm to the near-ticklish skin at the side of her breast. Her nipples tightened in anticipation of his clever mouth on those sensitive points, but he circled around the one without touching, lavishing her breast with sensation, teasing and stirring her to a frenzy.

With a cry of frustration, she seized his head trying to move him to her throbbing nipple—but he only laughed, husky and darkly amused, and took her other hand into his mouth. With infuriating patience, he repeated the performance on the other hand, giving each finger meticulous attention before making his way down her arm, exquisitely slow, maddeningly thorough.

By the time he reached her other breast, still not touching her nipples, Oria had enough. Her magic swirled in the air, raking light claws down his back as she clung to his shoulders. "Lonen," she panted, half in plea, half in warning.

He raised his head to stare her down, his face set in ridged lines of intense arousal, eyes flinty with determination. "No tricks, sorceress, or I'll stop."

"Don't you *dare*," she breathed, lifting her breasts to him, torn between begging and berating him.

He surveyed her with a molten stare, taking advantage of her arched back to slide his hands beneath and hold her there, draped over them. "In time, sweet. But only if you're good. No magic."

With supreme effort, she withdrew the mental claws, drawing the magic back into herself—which only made her feel more like exploding. "Be quick about it," she said through gritted teeth, "or I'm liable to tear the palace apart before I realize it."

He tsked, gently chiding. "You wanted to practice control."

She growled in frustration, choked off when he pressed a deep kiss to the hollow at the center of her collarbones, then licked her, in one long, hot and slick caress down between her breasts all the way to the top of her pubis. He lingered there, dipping his tongue into her belly button, holding her in a firm grip as she writhed and mewed.

A wail escaped her when he flipped her onto her belly. "Every bit of you, Oria," he reminded her in that sensual, graveled voice, gathering her hair and draping it to the side to expose the back of her neck. "You might as well resign yourself."

"You're so cruel," she whimpered, undulating with need as he pressed his mouth to the nape of her neck.

He sank his teeth into the thicker muscle where her shoulder met her throat, and she sobbed at the intensity of it. "Yes," he murmured, licking that spot, gentling her, then nipping at the skin along her spine on his way back up to her nape. "And you're all mine to do with as I will."

She moaned in resignation, letting him play his games, taunting and teasing her as he tasted every bit of her. As he made his way down her back, she lost all sense of time, of the edges of herself. Becoming only her skin and the unending sensations of his hot mouth and raking hands. She didn't protest as he continued past her bottom down her legs, to her toes. The backs of her knees, the hollows of her ankles, the tender arches of her feet, all quickened to his caresses, each dissolving her a little more.

She'd gone blind and deaf, insensate to everything but the dark magic he worked on her body. So when he kissed his way up her inner thighs, she only groaned, unable to bear any more, unable to resist.

When he spread her wide and put his mouth on her sex, she climaxed in a wrenching convulsion that had her tearing at the bed cover. She screamed, spine arching and head thrown back, and Lonen held her plunging hips in his hands, tongue an incredible sensation on her most delicate tissues.

Though he wasn't done with her, licking her through the orgasm, prolonging it, driving her still higher. When she neared peak again, he slid into her, and put his mouth on her nipple, sucking hard as he pinched the other.

Beyond the ability to make sound, she fully and completely shattered, becoming shards of starlight, swallowed in the blackness of night.

ORIA TRIED TO keep to a smooth pace as she made her way down to the dungeons. With every movement, however, each set of stairs she descended, aches and twinges reminded her of Lonen's vigorous lovemaking. He'd wrung her dry, seemingly inexhaustible himself.

The ribald remarks she'd heard the Destrye calling to each other about women walking funny in the morning kept echoing in her head. Apparently, they were based at least somewhat on reality. Though she'd experienced penetration before, nothing had prepared her for her husband's extremely well-endowed efforts. To make matters worse, when she'd commented on it, he'd only looked terribly pleased with himself and not sympathetic at all. Men.

"But you're happy?" Chuffta asked.

"Oh yes," she reassured him. *"Just sore and tired—and not willing to give Lonen any reason to expand his already big head."*

They hadn't slept much at all—just naps here and there—because every time she stirred, it seemed to awaken his insatiable hunger for her. Not that she minded. She'd known from their first wedding night that Lonen was a creative, sensitive, and generous lover—totally at odds with his barbarian mien—but she hadn't quite expected the intensity of being skin to skin with him. Or what access to her skin allowed him to do to her. He'd promised to consume her and she indeed felt entirely as if she'd been chewed up and left boneless.

"Perhaps you should sleep more," Chuffta offered solicitously. *"Or see a healer."*

"I don't need a healer." She mentally laughed, and also cringed, at the thought of telling even Baeltya about it. The thought of Vycayla somehow becoming involved…. No, no, no. *"I'm fine, really. I got used to riding a horse after all, and this is—"* She cut herself off, realizing how Lonen would laugh his ass off at that analogy.

"Why is that so funny?"

"It's a human thing. Listen along as I work with Nolan, all right? Just anything you notice." She nodded at the guard who unlocked the door for her to enter the lowest level of the dungeon. In better times, Lonen had told her as they curled together sleepily, a newly married couple could be expected to stay in their rooms for days—or even go off together some-where—and he offered for them to take a day or two. But she

hadn't needed to read his mind to know that, as much as part of him yearned to closet himself with her, he also itched to get after the business of the realm.

In truth, she should start learning her responsibilities as queen, but Lonen had preempted that impulse by telling her that her priority should be dealing with the sorcerous Báran taint in Nolan and his men. He hadn't said aloud, but they both knew that the first priority for Dru and the Destrye was planning for the inevitable next attack.

Or, rather, forestalling that possibility by taking the war to Bára.

"Do you think we will—go back to Bára and attack them?"

"Strange to think about, hmm?" Strange, indeed, to consider how she'd once stood at the balustrade of her high tower and looked out over the desert, straining for news of the battle she couldn't see. Now she'd be the enemy. But not to destroy Bára. No: to save it.

Nolan's ranting echoed down the tunnel of the corridor, the volume of it seeming to make the torches flicker, though Oria knew that shouldn't be possible. Adjusting her barriers, she steadied herself as she came around the last corner. As usual, he paced his cell, waving hands in the air as he raged.

Also as usual when Oria wasn't there, Natly perched on the stool. She seemed to be trying to talk to Nolan. She didn't hear Oria's approach immediately and started when Oria called out a hello, by way of warning. Glancing over her shoulder and quickly away, Natly brushed at her face. When she met Oria's gaze, her defiant one glistened still with tears.

"I'm surprised you're out of bed already. Your Highness," she added, a beat too late for true courtesy, not quite enough to be insolent.

Oria figured she'd be none too polite to a woman she knew

had just crawled wobbly-kneed out of Lonen's bed—more likely she'd be inclined to murder—so she ignored the slight. "I have work to do," she replied with a calming smile and gestured at Nolan. "Any changes?"

Natly bit her lip. The Destrye woman always groomed herself beautifully, fit for the queen she longed to be, so her lips were painted in crisp lines of glossy crimson, her dark eyes artfully highlighted with cosmetics, and her black hair piled in an artful tumble of curls and jewels. Oria was glad the ladies assigned to her had insisted on braiding her hair—adding the gold circlet—dressing her in a new gown and decorating her with subtle cosmetics and discreet jewelry. She wore her wedding cloak. The silk-lined emerald satin was heavy enough to keep her warm in the pervasive chill of the palace without her needing to expend magic to warm herself, but it was a better weight for indoors than the shadowcat fur cloak. Lonen had noted that her wearing Arill's colors would help establish Oria in her new role, too.

Lonen had similarly girded himself for the day ahead, and there had been something companionable and intimate in their shared ritual of donning their costumes as rulers.

And in the knowing that she'd return to him at the end of the day and remove it all again. Had she thought herself sexually exhausted? Apparently not, because the thought of what might occur once night fell had her flushing in anticipation.

Natly noted the blush, narrowing her eyes knowingly. Lonen had likely polished all those bed skills, those many clever tricks of his, with this woman. Once that realization might have made Oria jealous, but not now. To have had Lonen in her bed and lost him…Oria could only feel sorry for Natly, which the Destrye woman would not abide.

"I think he's worse," Natly finally said, her tone far less brash, and Oria recalled herself to the important matters at hand. Natly even stepped aside, not quite offering Oria the courtesy of acknowledging her rank, but making way for them both to observe Nolan. "I stayed until late last night and have been here a few hours. I don't think he's slept at all."

Nolan seized the iron grate barring the cell, shouting incoherently, eyes glassy and wild.

"Did *you* sleep much?" Oria asked without thinking, then wished she could take back the inconsiderate words.

"I couldn't," Natly bit out, her voice and spiky emotions daring Oria to say anything more.

"Nolan is fortunate in your devotion," Oria said instead.

That threw Natly off course, and she paused, reeling back whatever words she'd been poised to hurl at Oria. She gazed at Nolan with a strange expression on her face, her emotions a tangible snarl of worry, anger, fear—and love?

"I loved him once," Natly said, confirming it. "Long ago. Forever ago, it feels like. He didn't love me, but at least he wanted me." Rather than the brash, confidently aggressive woman Natly had presented herself as before, she sounded small in that moment, even forlorn. "Even after he returned, and Lonen… was with *you*, I offered to be his lover—we'd always been good together that way—and he ignored me. As if that part of him had died. I hate what's become of him."

The way Nolan's once-handsome face contorted in his insane ire, spittle flecking his filthy beard, Oria didn't blame Natly a bit. She couldn't imagine seeing Lonen in such a state. And it was all her people's fault. Whoever had turned Nolan's mind—Oria's brother Yar or someone else—the guilt belonged to Bára.

"I'm going to help him," she told Natly, setting the resolve in herself as she said the words. "Maybe you should go rest. Come back later and—"

"You can give me orders," Natly said in a flat, malicious voice, all softness gone. "Because you are Queen of Dru now, and I'll obey. I won't give you reason to have me exiled for disloyalty. But don't pretend that you care a fig for me." She gathered her skirts and strode off in a brisk, athletic stride, jewelry chiming as she went.

"*Good riddance, I say,*" Chuffta remarked. "*She makes my ears hurt.*"

"*How can she make your ears hurt when you can't literally hear her.*"

"*I don't know. She just* does.*"

Privately Oria had to agree that the area felt calmer without Natly's prickly presence—which was saying something given Nolan's noisy behavior—though she also felt petty thinking it. Natly had suffered a great deal and lost her planned future. Oria should try to be more generous in her thoughts. She sat on the stool Natly had vacated and cleared her mind. Lately she'd been drawing on the sensations of flying to get there, evoking that calm, in-the-moment peacefulness of simply existing in the world. Back in Bára, Chuffta had helped her meditate by guiding her into trances that at least mimicked *hwil.*

Now she found that she could slip into that state—not *hwil,* which never had made sense to her—but a place of being, in the most profound and basic sense; a point of equilibrium, a still, quiet place she'd found in the inferno of the derkesthai cavern. Lonen's delicious torment had brought her to a similar place, one where she accepted the flow of existing without trying to control it. As if she had immense wings like Chuffta's, she soared on the currents of the wild magic.

Once those unpredictable currents had destabilized her, dragging her under and drowning conscious thought, driving her nearly insane. When she'd begun using the ancient mask of her ancestress, which she and Lonen had dug out of the unnamed sorceress's tomb, the magical artifact had focused and exacerbated the effect—to the point that it had nearly killed her. Lonen had overreacted, wanting to take it from her. But after the trials with the derkesthai, Oria felt confident she could use the mask effectively, with no damage to herself.

But she kept the mask out of Lonen's sight anyway. He hadn't mentioned it since they had found each other again— possibly with so much on his mind, he'd forgotten about it, or thought she'd lost it in the molten lakes of the derkesthai caverns—so she hadn't brought it to his attention. If they took the war back to Bára, then she would need to have the mask in hand. She and Lonen could fight about it then.

For the moment, she'd hold the mask in reserve. She held on to that steady core of balanced self, sailing with the magic, absorbing it into herself and becoming one with it. Not helplessly tossed about, but integrated.

One with the flow of the magic of the world, she moved the flow of it with her. If she let herself, she could spend hours distracted by the rivers and streams of different kinds of magic, each with its own particular quality. They'd be different scents or flavors, if magic was chemical. Or colors, if magic flows were a visible thing. They'd be different notes in a song if magic could be heard, the melodies and harmonies related to the source of that magic.

Gradually, however, she'd begun to learn to accept magic as its own thing. She didn't perceive it with the same parts of herself that smelled, saw, or heard things. It could be that the part of herself that sensed, drew in, and manipulated magic had nothing to do with her physical body at all. Thus, comparing her magical senses to physical ones would only lead her down false paths.

She'd been mulling this, contemplating it in the last days while flying on Chuffta and distracting herself from anticipating the wedding. That had been a good event, no doubt about it, but it felt good to have their personal lives settled, and their political ones, too. Now she could concentrate on her sorcery.

And her first big project: finding the magical corruption in Nolan.

Removing it would be the second ambitious project.

In the still place, she shut out her physical senses, aware only of the world formed entirely of magic. There, Nolan's shouted epithets didn't exist, nor did the hard stool or the chill, dank air of the dungeons. Even she didn't exist, exactly, nor did Chuffta, but they were together, swimming in an endless sea of magic.

"Or flying."

"Yes. I'm going to look in a different place this time. Tell me what you notice."

When she'd tried before, she'd looked into Nolan's mind, the way she read Lonen's thoughts or sensed the wordless images from Buttercup. With no time to spend with Nolan the day before, and lots of time to mull while all the ladies decorated her for the wedding, she'd realized that Yar—or whatever sorcerer had worked this magic to poison Nolan's thoughts—would predict that Oria could read them.

Till now she'd thought that Yar assumed her to be dead. A reasonable assumption, since no sorceress had survived long outside of the walls of her city and its sustaining source of sgath. She herself had thought she'd die. Likely she would have, if not for Lonen's stubborn determination to save her life, and his ridiculous optimism that he could thwart everything the Bárans knew about how sgath and the wild magic worked.

Never mind that he'd turned out to be right.

Oria had realized that whatever opened Nolan's mind to Báran influence could be a two-way connection. The golems could also operate that way. The silicate constructs were given packets of sgath to animate them and instructions to follow, but Oria could receive and well as send through her magic portals. Surely a sorcerer could, too. Which might mean that Yar had been aware that Oria had survived ever since the Golems attacked her and Lonen in the desert. If so, he might've gained even more information once Nolan found them at the borders of Dru.

Worst of all, he might now know everything Nolan knew about Dru and the Destrye.

That realization changed nothing—they could hardly prepare for attack any more than they had—so she hadn't mentioned this possibility to Lonen. Not yet. Not until she tested her theory. If Yar had anticipated that Oria would read Nolan's thoughts, then the taint lay somewhere Yar believed Oria couldn't access.

So, this time, instead of looking in Nolan's chaotic thoughts—an unpleasant experience, regardless—she looked at other parts of his being. Particularly the masculine aspects. Yar wouldn't easily relinquish his ideas of the superiority of male grien and the sorcerers who wielded it. Even though he'd personally witnessed Oria using grien, active magic supposedly beyond the reach of women, that self-absorbed and self-congratulatory ego of his would blind him to the truth. She was gambling that he'd consider anything male beyond her ability to comprehend.

Sifting through Nolan's masculine nature, she found it grounded in the physical body. From there the personality stemmed, partly shaped by the physical, partly by the non-physical. To her surprise, she found that the eternal aspect of Nolan—that which had existed before his birth and which would move on following the death of his body—was neither male nor female.

"This could explain why you can access both sgath and grien," Chuffta noted quietly, observing along with her. *"You've found that the world of magic exists beyond the physical. If you are not your body, then your use of magic is neither male nor female."*

"Balance in all things," she remembered the Great One trying to explain. *"Finding the point of equilibrium could mean between masculine and feminine also."*

He agreed, wordless in their connection in this space.

She moved into the parts of Nolan's identity where his sense of himself as a man resided. And there, she found what she sought.

~ 7 ~

"**E**XPLAIN THAT AGAIN**," Lonen told Oria, wondering to himself if he'd heard correctly.

Oria huffed out a breath in exasperation, which made her full breasts—nicely displayed in the pretty gown her ladies had dressed her in—rise and fall enticingly. Not something that helped his concentration on the conversation. When Oria had asked to have their midday meal in private, in their chambers, and he'd assumed she had more sex on her mind. But no, she wanted to talk about his *brother*.

"I've already explained it twice," she replied crisply, narrowing her eyes at him. "Focus on what I'm saying, not on my breasts."

He grinned at her, unrepentant. "They're beautiful breasts, and delicious. I'd like to have my mouth on them."

"I shouldn't have suggested a private meal here," she said with rueful resignation. "I wanted a confidential conversation with the king, not a tryst with the man."

"All right, all right," he conceded. With an effort, he wrenched his mind from salacious fantasies and thought through what Oria had explained about Nolan's state of mind. At least thinking about his crazed brother and his backstabbing treachery, regardless of the reasons for it, had the salutary effect of quenching his desire.

"So, if I understand correctly, you found magic that you associate with that of the Báran sorcerers, though not Yar specifically, and it's attached to Nolan in his male sexuality?"

Oria beamed at him like he was a prize student. "You *were* listening! That's exactly what I'm saying."

Hmm. Though it still didn't make any sense. "Are you asking me to cut off my brother's balls?"

She burst out laughing. "No! Not a bit of it. That's the physical. I'm talking about the non-physical."

"Some of us, like your loving husband," he said, pointing his eating knife at himself, "have only the physical world to deal with."

"Is that right?" she replied archly. "What about Arill?"

"She's a goddess."

"Does She exist physically?"

"Well, no, but—"

"What about the healers in Arill's service, like Baeltya and your mother—is their healing magic a physical thing?"

She was making his head hurt. What came of marrying a sorceress, no doubt. "Yes," he decided. "Because I can feel it, therefore it exists physically."

"Can you touch the healing magic? Smell it, see it, hear it?"

"No," he conceded. "But it obviously exists, because it has an effect."

"Exactly," she pounced on the point. "You feel the effects of the healing, but not the magic that induces the healing, because that exists on a non-physical plane of reality."

He nearly asked if it counted as "reality" if it didn't exist physically, but Oria looked so earnest in her explanation, and so excited about her discovery, that he didn't have the heart to tease her about it. He also still didn't know what tree she was climbing. "Oria, my love, can you indulge your barbarian of a husband and reduce this discussion to what actions we can take? Whatever we need to do to fix Nolan, I want to do."

"Well, that's just it," she said thoughtfully. "I'm not sure we should."

He reined in the surge of anger that she'd suggest such a thing—especially since her calm expression and sparkling gaze held no hint of malice or revenge. "Then what?" he asked simply, pushing his empty plate aside and leaning his forearms on the table.

She hesitated, a line forming between her brows. "You won't like this part."

Oh, wonderful. As if he'd liked any of this. "Say it anyway," he said, as calmly as he could.

As she explained her theory, however, that the magically implanted control that guided Nolan's thoughts and actions might actually be a conduit that linked everything Nolan experienced back to a sorcerer in Yar, his rage grew. His fingers itched for his iron battle-axe, leaning against the wall nearby, even though this particular enemy—this non-physical *thing* Oria spoke of—couldn't be hacked apart. It would ease him to have the axe in his hands. He'd agreed to wear the crown of Dru again, but nothing could make him take up his father's sword, the one Nolan had nearly killed him with. He trusted the battle-axe like he trusted his warhorse, Buttercup, like he trusted Oria.

"Lonen." Oria leaned on the table, too, copper gaze intent, a whisper of her essence in his mind drawing him out of his dark thoughts.

He blinked away the red haze. "So he's a spy. All the time that he accused you of being a spy for the enemy, accused *me* of being subverted by you, under your control, *he* was the one. All this time, working to destroy us."

She smiled, crooked and close-lipped, both wry and sorrowful. "It's a clever way to divert suspicion—accuse others of the very thing you're guilty of."

"I could kill him for this," Lonen snarled, all those conversations with Nolan rolling through his head, the plans to repair the aqueducts, their strategy to plant crops in widely varying places and scatter livestock herds so that if one portion met with destruction, they might still have another… all known to the enemy. A few of the Trom dragons deployed to the right places and within the space of an hour they could lose everything, be utterly and finally destroyed.

Oria covered his hand with hers, small and delicate, but fiercely strong. "It's not his fault, Lonen. Don't kill him for that."

"Right. I'll just cut off his balls then," he suggested, intending it as a joke, though it came out far too lethal sounding.

"He didn't consciously betray you," Oria insisted.

"You're sure of that?"

She nodded, absolutely serious. "It's not in his mind at all. Probably to him it feels like he's in a dream. If he's aware at all."

"He acted like himself, for a while."

"Do you want to know what I think they did to him, what happened?"

"Will I understand?" he retorted grimly.

Oria laughed and rolled her eyes. "You may be a hulking brute of a barbarian, husband of mine, but I happen to know what a sharp mind you have inside that thick skull. Of course you'll understand, as long as you're not thinking about sex instead," she added with a teasing note.

Sex, and happy topics in general, had fled far from his mind. He'd grown used to sorcery, being around Oria—but like her, the magic she embodied seemed full of light and the beauty of nature. Things he understood and loved about the world. This conversation… it reminded him of how he used to feel about Báran magic, ground under by the odious stuff. "All right." He sighed, bracing himself. "Explain."

"What would you be thinking about if I came over there, knelt down, and took your cock in my mouth?" she asked.

He paused, disconcerted—and immediately aroused. They hadn't done that yet, her mouth, hot, wet, and tight on his intimate flesh. "I thought you didn't want me to think about sex."

"Where did your mind go just now?" she asked seriously, not flirting at all.

"You know perfectly well, sorceress," he growled at her. "Since you can read my mind, you know how much I want that."

"Could feel it? Imagine me on my knees in front of you?"

His cock had grown so hard he had to adjust it, giving her a wry glance as he did. "Yes."

"Even though it wasn't real," she pressed the point.

"Even so," he agreed.

"So, even though we're having a very serious conversation about something critically important to you on several levels, with a few words I managed to divert your thoughts to something else entirely."

"Something that's never entirely far from my thoughts to begin with," he pointed out. Especially with her in the room. Perhaps one day this hunger for her would relent, but the day after their wedding? Not likely. "Is there a point to this game of yours, Oria?"

"Don't get testy with me. Of course there's a point. I played on your male sexuality to influence the direction of your thoughts, and by saying only a few words."

"A few extraordinarily enticing words," he felt he had to say.

"I acknowledge I had a good idea of which words to use," she replied with a feline smile. "Now: imagine what a clever person with a good idea of which words to use, *and* powerful magic at their command, could do to a man's thoughts."

Understanding dawned, clearing his muddy head. "So, every time Nolan thought about sex..." He trailed off, the enormity of that hitting him.

"Not even thought about it," Oria replied in all seriousness. "Just felt the urge. How many times a day do you feel a sexual urge, even if you don't give it much thought?"

Every fucking minute of every day, with Oria near. "Arill save us," he whispered.

"I realized this in part because of something Natly said, that Nolan used to be a vigorous and enthusiastic lover, but after he returned, she said it was like that aspect of him had died. It occurred to me that maybe it wasn't dead and instead pointed in a different direction."

"So when he felt any urge, his mind went to, what, betraying the Destrye?"

She shrugged a little. "Of that I can't be too sure. The spell is complex and finely wrought, like a spiderweb of metal wrapped around his sexual being. Probably the suggestions are simple and easily followed. Like commands you'd give Buttercup, so as not to confuse him."

"Don't be insulting my warhorse," Lonen shot back, not angrily, but relieved that he could make a joke during this horrible conversation.

Oria smiled back, looking relieved by his levity, too. "No insult to Buttercup intended. I just mean that if you could give

Buttercup instructions to go off and accomplish some task by himself, wouldn't you want those directives to be pretty straightforward? Clear tasks, that could be adapted to circumstances, but nothing so complex that the plan would fall apart if some component changed."

An idea of that formed in his head. "So nothing so vague as 'destroy the Destrye,' but maybe 'become king.'"

She nodded. "At any cost. And there seems to be a kind of intensification built into the spell, so that if he doesn't succeed, it drives him to try harder."

"The more he's thwarted, the harder he tries."

"Exactly." She looked grim as he felt now.

"But, if he can't try, if he's prevented, wouldn't that—" He cut himself off, unwilling to say the words.

"Drive a man mad," Oria said softly. "That's what I'm guessing is happening to him."

Horrifying to imagine. He stared at Oria. Surely she couldn't be so cruel as to want that for Nolan. Even his own craving for revenge, his certainty that Nolan deserved death for his treachery, had evaporated with these revelations. "How can you suggest leaving him that way?" he got out. "Would you leave him to go so mad that he can never be healed?"

"Oh!" Oria's eyes rounded in shock—and a reassuring tinge of horror at the picture he painted. "No, that's not what I meant at all. You think I would want that for your brother?"

"Then what?" he ground out. "Just tell me."

"I'm sorry," she said. "I—"

"There's your one for the day," he said, reaching across the table to take her hand in an apology of his own.

She returned the smile, acknowledging the days when they'd each apologized to the other so much that they'd set a rule to limit it to one apology for each per day. They'd moved past that at some point in the last weeks, finally easy enough with each other that they weren't forever worrying about their own failings. Perhaps that indicated they'd become more confident in themselves, too. Certainly Oria seemed to have done. She spoke about her abilities as a sorceress in a way she hadn't before.

And Lonen himself had grown, no longer secretly believing himself a fraud and imposter on the throne. He'd claimed the throne through his own abilities and determination, as well as the vagaries of fate. He'd be the best ruler for the Destrye that he could be.

"I think we should let Nolan believe he's succeeding in his goals," Oria said, as if that made perfect sense. When he frowned at her, trying to follow why she'd suggest something so outrageous, she continued. "If he believes he's following directives, the loop of magic driving him should ease off. With every goal accomplished, he should return to a more sane state of mind."

"Are you saying we should… make him king?"

Oria shook her head, then nodded. "I think we should let him *believe* he's king. You have a palace full of subjects utterly loyal to you. If we tell everyone to play along, we can all pretend he's won, that he's actually king—and then we can observe what else he does, and thus learn what the Bárans have planned."

A sneaky plan—perhaps an exceedingly clever one—but fraught with possibilities for failure. "But if he's also relaying information back to Bára…" He said as he thought it through.

"Then we can feed him, and thus them, the information we want them to have."

"If they already know I won the challenge, that I'm king and you're officially my queen, and that Nolan has been

imprisoned, won't they be suspicious if that suddenly changes?"

She held up a slender finger, eyes glowing with excitement.
"Aha! But *does* Nolan know that? Think back. He knows he
gravely wounded you in the duel, and that you both fell. Your
iron axe disrupted some of the magical connection, plus you
knocked him unconscious, so they can't know what happened
after that except that he woke up healed and imprisoned in the
dungeons."

"He saw me come find you there, though."

"Yes, but he was ranting, not listening. I'm not convinced
he noticed you at all. Even if he did, you weren't wearing the
crown or carrying your father's sword."

"He will have noticed you, however. You've been with
him a great deal."

"Yes, but what will Yar and his cronies make of that? They
won't believe I have magic capable of cracking theirs."

"You defeated Yar in that contest of your magics."

"Yes, but Yar thinks I cheated and that Gallia failed him.
She should've been the perfectly harmonious match for his
magic—and she was powerful, in her home of Lousá—but
Báran sgath was unfamiliar to her. You've met Yar. Which is
more likely—that he'll honestly see that his magic is no match
for his sister who failed to master even basic *hwil*, much less
magics he could do by fifteen, or that he'll decide to blame
everyone but himself?"

She had a point there. Her brother had all the brash hubris
of youth. Even with maturity, Yar might not gain the strength
of character to examine his own weaknesses—and to recognize
others possessed abilities he lacked.

"All right," he said slowly. "Let's say we release Nolan
from his cell. Why would he suddenly go from being a

prisoner to the throne?"

Oria leaned in, expression full of wicked delight. "*We* won't release him. His loyal co-conspirator Natly will free him."

"And I'll be in the dungeon cell in his place?" Lonen folded his arms, trying to look forbidding. In truth, he could see where she was going with this. The plan had possibilities.

"No dungeon cell for you, my king," she replied with a twinkle of amusement.

"Won't Nolan notice if I'm wandering around, not defeated?"

"He might, if you were in Dru."

"I won't be in Dru?"

She shook her head from side to side, terribly pleased with herself. "Neither of us will be. Because while Yar and the rest of the Báran sorcerers are preoccupied with Nolan finally being on the throne of Dru uncontested, executing whatever their next instruction is, we will be leading the army to attack Bára."

He sat back in his chair, the possibilities opening up, laying themselves out neatly. "We muster the warriors and begin shifting the troops to just beyond Bára. Once we're clear of Arill City, Natly frees Nolan in a brave coup. A skeleton staff of warriors puts up a token fight, then declares loyalty."

"Exactly. We wouldn't need a lot of people to make it convincing—just enough to create verisimilitude where Nolan can observe. We leave trusted friends to observe him and notify us of his initiatives. Meanwhile, Yar and his cronies are lulled into complacency, thinking all is handled here until they can complete their conquest at leisure."

"The farther away we are, the longer it will take for anyone staying behind to notify us of Nolan's actions if he does something truly detrimental to Dru," he pointed out, not really arguing but mentally covering the logistics. "And taking an army on campaign in winter is difficult."

"I don't know much about that," she conceded, "but I have three thoughts. One is that pulling all of the warriors out of Arill City would relieve the housing and food problems, making it more likely the rest of the population can make it to spring."

"Not if we provision the army with the remaining food supplies."

"If we enlist your mother in this plan, we could ask for some of their supplies to provision the army. That was my second thought."

She had a cannier brain for this kind of planning than he'd have predicted. "And the third?"

"We travel through the tunnels."

~ 8 ~

ORIA RATHER SAVORED Lonen's astonishment at that suggestion—though the surprise quickly cleared from his face, replaced by shrewd analysis as he worked out the logistics with all the experience of his warrior's mind.

"The tunnels, huh?"

"Yes. Nolan said he and his men traveled from under Bára to the edge of the forests of Dru before emerging to travel the rest of the way overland."

Lonen stroked his chin, considering. "It could work. We know the tunnels are big enough to accommodate a warrior on horseback, though a large company will have to be strung out for leagues."

"Send warriors in small groups, one after the other."

He grunted at that thought. "We could do that, start sending the battalions most ready to leave as soon as possible to secure the entrance to the tunnels and begin sending warriors through. Nolan might not be willing to tell us where that was, however."

"Two things." Oria held up two fingers in demonstration. She'd had time to work on the details of her plan while she waited for Lonen to get free of business and join her for lunch. "The warriors who traveled with him will know, and if that becomes a problem, then I can look in Nolan's mind."

"I can see a problem right now," Lonen said with a frown, tapping his knuckles on the table. "What if those men have the same magical corruption? If they're spies also, then—No?"

He broke off as she shook her head. "I've checked all the ones in custody. None of them have any taint of Báran magic."

"You're sure?"

Oria restrained a sarcastic reply. "Yes, I'm sure. Once I found the magic binding Nolan, I checked those of his men in custody—falsely imprisoned, in light of this information, I might point out—and they don't have it. I wondered why I couldn't find anything different about them, but that's the answer. Only Nolan was tampered with."

"That doesn't mean that's true for those men we haven't located for you to examine," he countered. "Perhaps they're evading capture because they *have* been tampered with and want to be free to spy and conduct their sabotage efforts."

"*Or,*" she returned, "maybe they're evading capture because, oh, I don't know, maybe they don't want to be *imprisoned in the dungeons.*"

Lonen narrowed his eyes in a granite glare. "Destrye warriors are accustomed to hardships of all kinds—and to obeying their king."

Oria gave him a look of disbelief. Why was he being so obstinate? "Oh, you mean like you did? When Nolan wore the crown and ordered you imprisoned by the palace guard, did you meekly obey?"

"Of course not!" he snapped. "That was entirely different."

"Different why?" she asked sweetly, letting his anger wash over her, sampling it.

Emotions, it turned out, were another form of intangible energy. People sensed other people's emotions through physical cues—facial expressions and body movements, the sound of the voice, perhaps even a scent, like wolves smelling fear. Oria had always known that other people's emotions affected her—the stronger the emotion, the greater the effect. But she'd always been sadly at the mercy of them, which was why she'd lived alone atop her tower in Bára, to spare her the draining miasma of the people living in the city.

Now, with her growing mastery of magic, being able to perceive the flows of energy in all its various forms, she'd discovered that emotions were a form of magical energy—a kind that every person seemed able to manifest, whether they harnessed that to conscious purpose or not.

"It *is* different, Oria," Lonen answered her needling through gritted teeth.

"Why are you so angry?" She followed the emotions to the thoughts behind them, sifting for the source. "No one expects you to be perfect, Lonen. It's all right to make mistakes. You imprisoned those men for just cause. Now we know there isn't one. Don't cling to the decision just because you don't want to admit an error."

"Reading my thoughts?" he asked, palms flat on the table.

"Yes," she replied candidly. "You've known from the beginning that I can. Even when I had little control of my magic, your thoughts and feelings have loomed large in mine. If you don't want me to, I can make an effort to close off those channels. All you have to do is say so."

His set expression softened, and he scrubbed his hands over his face, then through his hair, seeming surprised when his fingers snagged on the crown. Pulling it off, he set it beside him on the table. He gave her a wry smile. "It's a bit unsettling, how precise you've gotten at it."

"Part of mastering my magic overall," she agreed. "I'm getting more precise at all of those skills." When he didn't immediately reply, her stomach dropped. Stricken with fear that she'd misstepped, that she'd abused his trust, she asked. "Did I do wrong?"

"No." He looked up from the crown he'd been contemplating as if it held answers, took in her expression, then scooted back his chair. "Come here, love."

Gladly, needing the reassurance, Oria came around the table to settle on his lap, inside the circle of the arms he held open for her. He held her there a moment, then tipped up her chin and kissed her, long and sweet and loving. Heat billowed between them and she melted into it, relaxing against him. A knock on the door had him breaking off the kiss with a sound of regret.

"Your Highness," Alby discreetly called through the door. "I'm to remind you of the time."

"In a moment," he called back, and urged Oria to sit up straight on his knee again, then adjusting the fit of his crotch yet again, and with a rueful smile. "Arnon is waiting for me," he explained. "Unfortunately."

"There's tonight," she offered, hopefully.

"Always." He kissed her forehead. "And no, you didn't do wrong. It's good for me to have a sorceress wife who can glance into my mind and call me on my horseshit. But I want you to examine *all* of Nolan's men. If we can round them up."

"Release the ones in custody," she suggested, "and tell them to carry a message, along with a public proclamation, that these have been examined and absolved of any guilt, and the others can present themselves to be absolved also."

"Clever," he agreed, tugging on a lock of her hair. "If excessively civilized."

"Well, you could go around and bash everyone's heads in with your axe, if you'd prefer."

"I would certainly enjoy that more."

"Poor thwarted barbarian," she cooed.

He pinched her bottom, making her squeal. "I'll just have to take out my barbarous urges on my tame witch tonight."

"Oh, will you?" She tried to look menacing, but the immediate arousal at his words—and the fantasy he painted in his mind—had her breathy and aroused instead.

"Yes, but not now." He stood, easily bringing her with him with his casual strength, and set her on her feet. "It's a good plan, Oria. Let's set it in motion. Come with me to meet Arnon. We can tell him about it and maybe he'll have a solution to speeding up communication between us and those watching Nolan. I don't know how we're going to recruit Natly to the cause. Regardless, we can pick apart the details. Arnon is exceptional at finding flaws."

The face Lonen made as he said that had her laughing. She patted his cheek—gasping when he captured her hand and pressed a hot kiss to her palm, his eyes silvery as he watched her over their joined hands.

"You can thrash out the plan and I'll meet you later," she said, tugging her hand away and folding his kiss into her palm. "But I'll handle Natly."

"Oh you will, will you?" He raised his brows.

"Yes," she replied, with more confidence than she felt, but she suspected she knew exactly how to entice the Destrye woman to cooperate. "I'll see you at dinner."

"Are you going somewhere?"

"Indeed. I also have a solution to the communication problem."

"And that is?"

"I need to make sure I can pull it off. I'll tell you either way tonight. Will you trust me until then?"

He bent over and kissed her, a gentle brush of lips that held a world of longing. "Until the end of time, my love."

"Or at least until dinner," she quipped with a smile, and handed him his crown. "Don't forget this."

"As if I could," he replied in a dry tone, settling it on his head again.

"THIS IS FUN!" Chuffta said, as she emerged onto the rooftop platform. Gone were the wedding decorations, musicians, and beautifully dressed guests. Instead the area swarmed with Destrye working with a great clamor of tools. Some dismantling a section here, others building there. Every one paused to bow deeply as she passed, then immediately resumed work.

Lonen had said that Arnon had taken on the project of building onto the palace with great enthusiasm and determination, but the progress startled her. Chuffta waited on the specially reinforced section where he'd perched for the wedding ceremony—and the Destrye all seemed to be keeping half an eye on him—talons digging into the wood, looking as pleased as he sounded.

"Just don't sit too heavily," she cautioned him. Maybe it was her imagination that the platform sloped down slightly in his direction.

"How am I supposed to do that?"

"I don't know." Visions of the palace collapsing beneath them dashed through her mind. *"Think light."*

"Hurry up and I can be in the air," he replied grumpily. And needlessly, because she was already there.

Drawing on the magic, she created a harness of soft rope over his torso. Having done it several times already made it easier, as if the pattern settled itself into her mind, quickly accessed and recreated. It seemed to come from thin air, but that was an illusion. She'd pulled the fibers from the dead grasses beneath the snow cover on the forest floor. Her magical perception showed her all sorts of aspects of the world that she hadn't perceived before—like that even dead-seeming grasses retained life, and a tangible energy available to be woven into a new thing entirely.

It made sense, now that she knew. Now that her world had resettled into another way of perceiving and being. Bára had been built of stone, but the structures had a beingness of a sort she'd recognized since early childhood. The jewelbirds in her garden, the blossoms they fed from, the soil that nourished the flowers and the water that kept them alive, the stones of her tower—all of them had their own distinct *presence* and nature. All of it connected and needing balance.

It was all so much more complex than the two faces of Báran magical theory, far more manifestations than sgath and grien. And yet, simpler, too. Everything was part of every-thing.

She climbed up the rope steps of the ladder, settled herself, and fastened the straps.

"I won't drop you." Chuffta sniffed—mentally, and with a puff of flame—and leapt into the air, wings working furiously to lift them.

"I know, darling." She stroked his neck. *"But this is good practice for us. If we encounter the Trom dragons in battle, or spells from the city sorcerers, then you'll need to be concentrating on dodging and flaming—not staying level so I won't fall off."*

"I shall flame them all!"

"Well, maybe not all."

"Spoilsport."

"No worries—there will be plenty of flaming." Probably far too much, but just as she'd had to pass through the crucible to emerge on the other side, so too would the Destrye and Bárans—and the Trom—to forge themselves into something new. Something once again balanced.

Chuffta winged toward the distant mountains, the ground flying past below. Incredible how swiftly they covered distances it had taken her and Lonen days to travel, even on fleet Buttercup. They flew over Vycayla's hermitage, a few white-robed women working the grounds pausing to shade their eyes against the bright winter sun, gazing up, and waving. Oria waved back, unsure if they could see her, a tiny rider atop Chuffta's immense form, but glad that the news of who she and Chuffta were had spread to them even in Vycayla's absence from the place.

A short time later, they passed over a steep, snow-capped ridge of peaks, and spiraled into the valley below. Even from her high vantage, the steaming hot pools glistened below in violent shades of lime, orange, and even violet. The fiery ones were mostly molten rock, welling up from the volcanic pits below ground. The others were water, but teemed with plants and animals that thrived in the intense heat, lending their strange colors to the broth of their isolated seas.

A triad of derkesthai flew toward them. The one in the lead had once been the largest derkesthai she'd ever seen—until she met their king, and then grown Chuffta to that size as one of her first great magical works.

"Hail Soldano," she projected. *"May we be welcome to the Colony?"*

"It seems you have might on your side," the colony guardian

replied, his mind-voice dry.

"Thanks to your and your king." She tried to sound meek and grateful. *"Though we would never bear ill-intentions toward those we call kin."*

"'Kin,' are we now? Then—"

"Leave off teasing them, Soldano." The derkesthai king's mind-voice thundered through hers. Chuffta didn't sound like that—thankfully—despite his equivalent size.

"The Great One is very old and powerful," Chuffta told her quietly, and privately. *"He sounds loud to me, too."*

"Approach already," the derkesthai king commanded. ***"I shall meet you outside the cavern mouth."***

Chuffta angled in that direction, the guardian trio wheeling to flank and escort them.

"Greetings Oria and Chuffta," one of the smaller derkesthai, the healer Tukcha said. *"You are both looking well. Especially you, Chuffta."*

Did Oria detect a flirtatious tone from Tukcha? Perhaps so, because Chuffta managed a preening neck curve, even with their rapid descent. Oria held on, glad to be validated in her prediction that she'd need the straps if Chuffta became distracted. She loved her Familiar, but he had a fiery and capricious nature. The wise sorceress recognized that and compensated for it.

"I am very big *now,"* Chuffta informed Tukcha, and Oria rolled her eyes at both his arrogant tone and statement of the obvious.

"So I observe," Tukcha replied mildly, but with enough amused reproof to make herself clear. *"And very handsome and powerful,"* she added, and Oria caught the wink in the healer's tone, probably meant just for the sorceress.

The derkesthai king emerged from the yawning cavern

mouth just as Chuffta landed on the stone apron before it. Set a bit above the level of the surrounding pools, the reception area provided a safe place for creatures not immune to flame—like herself—and also created a nicely defensible area for the derkesthai to repel unwelcome visitors.

"I didn't expect to see you again so soon, sorceress. Itching for another lesson?"

The king's thunderous laugh was close to painful, but Oria sat tall on Chuffta's shoulders, for once close to level with the big dragon's eyes. *"I believe I have plenty to work on for the time being, but thank you for the offer, Great One."*

"Hmm. I can't argue with that."

Oria very nearly preened like Chuffta at the implied compliment.

"Then why are you here, wasting my time?" the king demanded. *"I'm very busy."*

"Have an important nap by the lava lake scheduled?" she retorted with impertinence.

The great dragon's jaws opened in a lethal grin, green flames licking around teeth sharp as swords. *"As a matter of fact, yes. What do you want, sorceress?"*

Oria lifted her chin and met the dragon's gaze, and spoke aloud. "I've come to ask you and your people to join our army, to fight with the Destrye to save Bára and destroy the Trom."

~ 9 ~

"It's an audacious plan," Arnon commented after stroking his neat beard in silence a few moments. "I have to hand it to your Oria—she doesn't think small."

"She's your Oria, too," Lonen replied without rancor. "Your sister and your queen."

"Oh, yes, of course." Arnon waved that away, still deep in thought. "The communication is a problem."

"That's what I told Oria. She says she has a solution." Tired of sitting, Lonen rose from the study table and paced over to the window, one of the few in the palace proper, and pulled aside the hide covering it to keep the warmth in. The new apartments would have many windows, according to the designs Arnon had showed him. His canny brother hoped to bring back the transparent glass the Bárans forged from the sands surrounding the city—or, better still, with the knowledge to make it themselves. The Destrye knew plenty about forging metal, Arnon reasoned—why not sand?

"If we leave Nolan here, even as a fake king surrounded by people who know better, what's to stop him from summoning the Trom and their dragons to set fire to Arill City in our absence?"

"That would be bad," Lonen agreed. Where *had* Oria gone?

"Then we'd be a scattered people," Arnon continued, "with no base to speak of, our warriors at Bára and the rest of the Destrye isolated refugees."

"Our warriors would be at Bára, regardless."

"Yes, but even if we failed in the attack, the rest of our people would have a somewhat defensible place here. *Some* of our people would survive. At least they'd have a better chance together, with the moat and the stout walls of the palace between them and the golems and Trom. But not if Nolan has the power to undermine that."

"True," Lonen said. "But he won't have real power. We'll have people watching what he does, which will give us clues as to what the Bárans plan."

"Not if the people watching him can't communicate with us."

"I think I mentioned already that Oria has a way around that."

"What is it?"

Lonen shrugged. Still no sign of her. Easy to promise to trust. Not so easy to set aside his anxiety. He felt her presence, however, a bright and vital sun at the other end of the marriage bond—which felt stretched over a distance. Though…maybe less so that it had only a few minutes ago?

"It's a real flaw in the plan," Arnon argued, as if Lonen had denied it. "A horse and rider, even with fresh mounts at intervals and going top speed through the tunnels, would still take days. Overland would take even longer. Birds… maybe we could use birds, but they'd need at least a day each way, and we don't have messenger birds trained to find Bára. Besides, the Trom dragons could burn them from the air. And sending messenger birds could alert the Bárans to our movements and the element of surprise would be lost."

"Also true," Lonen answered, though Arnon hardly needed a response.

"I suppose we could just leave Mother in charge and trust her to use her best judgment. Alyx and her warrior women could serve as her personal guard and—"

"Alyx comes with us," Lonen interrupted. "So do *all* the warriors. Every Destrye who wishes to come and fight will be allowed—no, encouraged—to do so."

Arnon raised his brows. "You mean to stand by that idea, allowing the women to fight alongside the men?"

"I do." Lonen let the hide fall and turned to face his brother, leaning against the wall, arms crossed.

"It will cause problems. You know that our father decreed that—"

"I," Lonen interrupted in a flat voice, "am not father. I will not repeat his mistakes."

Arnon paused, considering. "You think his decision that the women shouldn't come to war with us, a war that seemed certain to end in doom—a debate argued long and hard with a great deal of input from all walks—was a mistake?"

Lonen held his brother's gaze. "Yes. It was a mistake. It resulted in a schism of our people at a time we could least afford to be divided, a fundamental division that reached all the way to the throne of Dru and resulted in our queen exiling herself from court."

"That was her decision, Lonen, and she—"

"Is it a 'decision' when a person chooses to live their life on their own terms rather than bow to having their rights taken away?"

Arnon pursed his lips. "That's a rather dramatic way of putting it."

"Is it? If a person wants to fight the enemy that threatens

their home, and someone else says they're not allowed to, that's taking away a fundamental human right. Even the lowliest of animals defend their territories."

"This is different, and you know it." Arnon threw up his hands. "Those women will endanger us by being on the battlefield."

"How so?" Lonen asked quietly.

"Don't play dumb, Lonen. You can talk change and progress all you like, but we are at heart still the barbarian people your Oria calls us. We haven't departed long from the days when women were legally property—ours to protect and cherish. If a woman is in danger on the battlefield, every man nearby will move to protect her. We won't be able to help ourselves. It's pure instinct. Would you punish a man for that?"

"Yes," Lonen replied. No question there. "If a Destrye warrior fails to follow orders, then yes, they will be punished. That's basic discipline every warrior learns along with how to properly hold a weapon."

"But instinct can override their—"

"Have you never had the instinct to run away instead of go forward in the crush of battle, Arnon? Have never had the impulse to do other than your commander ordered?"

"Well... yes, but—"

"There is no argument. We have military order because we have to override our instincts and impulses, for the greater good and strategy. You know that as well as I do, perhaps better."

Arnon raked a hand through his brown curls, stopping at the back of his neck and gripping it. "It's a hell of time to test the theory, Your Highness."

"Oh, *now* I'm 'Your Highness?'"

Arnon grinned back at him, releasing his tense posture and

shaking his head. "Absolutely. When I'm arguing with you, giving you my best advice, I'm your brother. When I'm certain you've decided, then I acknowledge that you are my king and have my unconditional support."

"Thank you," Lonen replied, voice unexpectedly rough with emotion. "For both the arguments and the support."

Arnon's smile took on a cocky bent. "Of course, I—what in Arill is *that* noise?"

Lonen had already spun to pull the hide from the window again, leaning out and craning his neck. The beat of thousands of wings thundered through the air, shrill reptilian calls echoing above the lower voiced shrieks of humans. For a panicked moment, he thought the Trom dragons might be attacking, but Oria's proximity—elated and triumphant—thrummed along the marriage bond.

And then he saw them. Arnon, wedged into the window beside him exhaled a giant breath of stunned awe. "Are those…?"

"Derkesthai," Lonen confirmed. "An entire colony. Oria brought them here."

Arnon cleared his throat. "For what purpose?"

Lonen pulled back, looping an arm around his brother's shoulders, letting the hide fall into place again. "Let's go find out."

ATOP THE PALACE, all but a few of Arnon's Destrye workers had fled from the onslaught of derkesthai. The smaller ones— the size Chuffta had been when he easily perched on Oria's shoulder—lit on the branches of Arill's tree. They looked oddly in place there, like exotic white flowers bringing the goddess's tree into bloom early. If Lonen let his gaze unfocus, the hundreds of bright green eyes could be new leaves amidst the living, shimmering wings, unfurling like waxy blossoms.

The derkesthai too large for the branches—fortunately no more than a handful—settled on the platform itself, and Chuffta landed on his accustomed spot, Oria on his back. She seemed to be unbuckling herself, then slid down Chuffta's leg and trotted toward them, an exultant smile on her face.

"I don't know that the struts will withstand this amount of weight," Arnon said, dropping to lie flat and look under the edge.

Lonen had eyes only for Oria. She looked to be wearing fighting leathers like the women warriors did, an adaptation of the standard male warrior's gear, scaled to size and reinforced in slightly different places to accommodate the female form. Only her leathers were a bright metallic copper that seemed to be embossed with scales. She gleamed in the late afternoon light like a derkesthai herself.

"What have you done, Oria?" he called, more forcefully than he meant to, overcome with both her feelings and his own.

She grinned at him, radiant with victory. "I've brought you reinforcements."

He opened his arms and she launched herself at him, wrapping her slender legs around his waist and returning his kiss with passion. Unable to resist, he slid a hand down to cup her small bottom, so enticingly clad in the soft leather. The embossed scales gave it an intriguing texture, and he squeezed, exploring.

She laughed, breaking the kiss. "Like them?"

"Yes," he answered. "Who do I have to thank for these?"

Her eyes danced with amusement. "Alyx provided the leathers, and my army of seamstresses adapted them to fit. Then I experimented a little with the color and design. I want something I can wear on Chuffta's back in battle that will suitably impress the Bárans when we accept their surrender."

"I understand the Bárans care about such niceties," he commented blandly.

"Oh yes," she replied in a mock serious tone. "Can you imagine what terrible terms we'd be forced into if we arrived at their gates dressed like barbarians?"

He scowled at her and bit her neck when she, giggling, dodged his retaliatory kiss. "Just so long as you don't agree to marry anyone else," he growled.

"If you two are finished," Arnon inserted, coming to stand beside them, "Your Highnesses, we really should relieve some of the weight on this platform before it collapses and takes the palace with it."

"Oops, sorry, Arnon." Oria glanced to the side, and the derkesthai, Chuffta included, took wing in a temporary blizzard. "I just wanted you to see them."

Arnon surveyed the departing… it seemed wrong to call them a flock, like birds. Perhaps a squadron? His brother cleared his throat. "It's an exhilarating sight, to be sure, but why are they here, Your Highness?"

Oria wiggled, so Lonen set her down. Even though she was shorter and far more delicate than the two of them, Oria stared Arnon down with all the regal arrogance of her heritage. "My dear barbarian brother of the heart, I can communicate mind-to-mind with these derkesthai."

Understanding dawned. "Over long distances?" he asked.

Oria held up her hands. She wore gloves of the same close-fitting, textured copper leather. "We need to test it, but I figure we can post the smaller derkesthai at intervals that match the range of their communication distance. The relay would be nearly instantaneous—at most a matter of minutes."

"Why only the smaller ones?" Arnon wondered, eyeing the many winged lizards festooning Arill's tree, preening and fluttering thin-membraned wings.

"First, because they can ride on your shoulder. I think all your officers should have one," she said to Lonen.

"We can't hear what they're saying," Arnon replied, bemused, as Lonen nodded at the wisdom of the plan.

Lonen clapped his brother on the shoulder. "You'd be surprised how much they can communicate non-verbally. Certainly they can alert you to problems or point you in a necessary direction."

"And defend you with flame," Oria added.

"I see." Arnon mulled that over, casting a glance at the struts underpinning the platform as they descended the steps. They looked fine to Lonen, but Arnon gestured at his foreman, who at least hadn't fled far, then pointed him at something. "Dare I ask what the big ones will be doing?"

Oria grinned, a lethal smile, full of teeth—and worthy of the most barbarous Destrye warrior woman. "They'll be in my aerial squadron. You and your warriors will handle the Báran city guard on the ground. If the Trom dragons arrive, we'll face them in the sky."

"I'M STILL NOT convinced this is the best idea," Lonen argued, fully aware of his hypocrisy—and relieved Oria hadn't been there that afternoon for the argument with Arnon about women in battle. What she didn't know, she couldn't call him on, and he made sure to push thoughts of that conversation down deep where she couldn't easily hear it. "There were a lot more Trom dragons at the Battle of Bára than I saw today of even moderately sized derkesthai."

"I'll be on Chuffta to lead the defense, so I'll be using magic. And don't forget the Great One." Oria turned her back and held up her hair so he could unlace the gown she'd worn to dinner. Another pretty one, though not half so alluring as those figure-hugging leathers had been. "He'll arrive when we're ready to depart. Until then he elected to stay warm by his lava lake."

"I'm surprised the others didn't do that, too."

She shrugged a little the loosening gown falling away more. "They were all curious and excited. How could I say no? But, speaking of warmth, did you—"

"Yes, yes," he interrupted. "I set men to clearing a swath of the moat. The derkesthai are all in there with a good supply of wood lighting their bonfires."

"Good idea," she admitted. "I wondered what Chuffta was talking about. It sounds like quite the party. It's not as if any golems could get past that lot."

He pushed the gown off her pale shoulders, indulging himself in savoring the texture of her skin. Softer than silk or velvet, that slight shimmery feeling of her magic coursing through her body, her skin enticed him to savor her more and more and more. He kissed the back of her neck, exposed with her hand still holding her hair out of the way, and she hummed with pleasure.

"I don't like the idea of you facing the Trom and their

dragons without me," he admitted, lips moving on her nape in a caress that made her shiver.

"You're going to say that, and after you managed to convince Arnon otherwise?" she countered, stepping away and putting her fists on her hips. Her expression was fierce, but the way her copper hair fell in a cloud around her, crackling with static and catching the firelight, her full breasts bare, small nipples pink and tight—she looked far too lovely and alluring. So much so that it took him a moment to catch up to what she'd said. Arill curse it.

"You read that in my mind?" he demanded. He'd have to get better about not thinking about things she could easily "overhear."

She smiled in triumph. "No. You actually are getting better at hiding thoughts you don't want me to 'overhear.' I read it in Arnon's mind. He kept going over the conversation in his head during dinner. Loudly. You really upset his tidy world."

Deciding he'd do better to distract his wife than argue with her, Lonen snagged Oria around her waist, threw her over his shoulder and carried her to the bed. "I think I'd rather upset your tidy world," he told her as she dissolved into shrieking laughter.

He tossed her on the bed, quickly ridding her of the rest of the gown. She stretched, slender arms over her head, her lovely body pale against her shining hair and the darker furs of their coverlets. Grabbing her ankles, he lifted a delicately arched foot, pressing a kiss to that spot he'd discovered undid her. She moaned, going languid in his grip, then tugged her foot free.

"Think again, Destrye," she said, kneeling up and crawling over the bed to him. Reaching for his belt buckle, she worked to undo it, glancing coyly up at him. "I believe I made a suggestion at lunch I should follow through on."

The memory had his already hard cock throbbing. He brushed a hand over her hair as she freed his cock and pushed his pants down. "Are you sure?" he asked, feathering fingers under her chin, coaxing her to look up so he could see her face.

She'd licked her lips, and they glistened full and wet, her eyes full of sensual desire. "Oh, yes, barbarian," she purred. "Tonight I get to torment you. Isn't that what a good tame witch does to appease her brutish captor?"

He began to reply in kind, but his sally choked off in his throat as her avid mouth closed over him, and his eyes rolled back in his head from the pure intensity of the sensation. Giving himself over, he let her plunder his body, wondering who in fact had captured whom.

~ 10 ~

"GOOD AFTERNOON, NATLY," Oria said from her seat at the prettily set table. "Would you like tea or wine?"

The Destrye woman eyed her with suspicion, her gaze then roving over the intimate salon with its dainty table for two. "I've lived here my entire life and I've never been in this room," she commented, hovering by the door, even though the lady who'd escorted her there had closed it discreetly.

"They call it the queen's salon," Oria replied easily. "I understand the Dowager Queen Vycayla rarely used it even before she withdrew to her hermitage, and it was closed off after that."

"Vycayla was never much for afternoon tea and sweets," Natly replied, giving those guilty items a scathing look. "I'm surprised she gave up her rooms entirely. What black magic did you have to work on her to accomplish that?"

Oria decided on wine, pouring them both some. "She called it a wedding gift, certainly a generous one. Possibly being confined here for several days by Nolan soured her on the place. She says she's happier at the temple and my ladies seemed delighted to fix up this little salon again. It works well for me as there are vanishingly few places in this palace where I can have a conversation. Come and sit." She added a tone of regal command, lest Natly continue to play the game of standing by the door.

After a beat—not hesitation, but a demonstration of insolence—Natly strolled to the table and sat. Taking up the metal goblet, she drank the excellent wine in one swallow, setting it down with a smile that was more of a sneer. Oria obligingly filled the goblet again, raising one brow in a dare.

If Natly wanted to get roaring drunk, Oria had plenty of wine and its effects would suit her objectives just fine. Natly, however, seemed to wise up and simply wrapped her hand around the cup, her jeweled nails flashing. "If you want to interrogate me, you'd do better with torture than wine." Natly threw the defiant words on the table between them like a warrior tossing a blade to their opponent, hoping they'll take it up in challenge.

Instead Oria picked up a cookie and nibbled it. Made from crushed nuts and a sugary syrup reduced from the sap of trees, the cookies had a lovely subtle sweetness unlike anything she'd had in Bára. "I don't."

Natly didn't change expression, or alter the hard stare from her dark eyes, but her thoughts stuttered from their determined path. Oria wasn't reading her, exactly—she hoped to keep that invasion as a last resort for dealing with anyone, except perhaps her husband, who deserved what he got—but when Natly was practically shouting her anger and jealousy, a change in the flow came through clearly. "You don't what, Your Highness?"

"Ah, you do know my title," Oria said, sipping her wine and taking another cookie. The flavors complimented each other well. "I didn't think you were too stupid to be making that mistake accidentally. I don't want to interrogate you," she continued smoothly when Natly opened her mouth to say something she'd likely be made to regret.

"Then why did you summon me, *Your Highness?*" she practically snarled.

Oria pushed the plate of cookies toward her, gesturing in demonstration. "Wine and cookies."

With an impatient huff, Natly took a cookie and ate it. Then drank down all of her wine in one swallow again. "There. May I be excused now, Your Highness?"

"No," Oria said in a tone hard enough to freeze Natly as she scooted back her chair. "You will stay until I excuse you. More wine?"

Natly gave her a long and burning look, then held out her goblet. "Might as well, since I'm trapped here."

Oria smiled genially, filling the goblet and topping off her own. Lifting a metal bell from the table, she rang it. "We'll need another carafe of wine, please," she told the lady who popped her head in. Once the door had closed again, Oria relaxed back in her chair. "I have a proposal for you, Natly."

"Our stallion Lonen isn't pleasing you in bed?" Natly opened her lushly lashed eyes wide in pretend shock. "I'm afraid the fault there is yours. He always satisfied me very well. Over and over. But then, I know a great deal about coaxing a man to peak performance—nothing a virgin could be expected to employ. I can't help you, however, as women hold no interest for me. Not enough cock." She smirked over her goblet.

Oria let her run on and wind down, waiting Natly out with amused placidity. One thing about being the magical runt of the litter with three brothers all far more proficient in magic than she, Oria had learned how to handle this kind of vicious needling. The bullies—Yar sprang to mind—fed off their victims' pain. Without a reaction, they ran out of steam. As Natly had, now fidgeting in the face of Oria's silence. Natly took a cookie and ate it, somewhat defiantly.

The silence between them stretched on, broken only by the lady delivering more wine. Oria thanked her and topped off Natly's goblet. She sat back and waited patiently. It was peaceful, after a fashion, especially with Chuffta off playing derkesthai games, practically giddy to have the company of his kind. And she'd given him a pass, since he always complained so bitterly that Natly hurt his ears.

"Fine," Natly snapped, folding her arms. "Since you'll clearly keep me imprisoned here until I listen to whatever ridiculous idea you have, Your Highness, tell me. What is your proposal?"

"I'm glad you asked," Oria replied with a polite smile, as if the interlude had never occurred. "This is hardly a prison. If it is, it's far more pleasant than the cell Nolan finds himself in."

Natly choked on her cookie crumbs, bending her head and thumping her chest. When she raised her eyes to Oria's, hers glittered with hatred—and perhaps a bit of respect. "Do you want me to say you've won—is that what this is about? Gloating is so petty."

Oria restrained the urge to comment that Natly would know. "You told me that you and Nolan used to be lovers. Do you love him still?"

With a sullen stare, Natly shrugged one shoulder, toying with her goblet. "Love," she scoffed. "What is it anyway? An occupation for adolescents."

"So you only offered your affections to Nolan and Lonen because you aspired to be queen?" And to Arnon and their older brother Ion before he took Salaya as his wife, from what Lonen had said.

"Is that what Lonen told you?" She lowered her gaze to her goblet. "It's easy for you to sneer at a woman like me, I imagine, to think that I only wanted to climb the tallest tree I could. But there's not much else for a woman of no family. I don't have *magic*. I have no connections, no property or wealth. All of that is gone."

"Lost to the Báran golems?" Oria made herself ask.

"Yes, long ago, when I was a girl. We used to be the wealthiest family in Dru, with fertile lands for ranching and farming. We even had a small township attached to the lands. Lots of water." She gave Oria a hate-filled stare. "It's desert now. And I have nothing to offer my children, if I ever manage to have any. So don't sit there in your Báran arrogance and judge me for trying to be queen."

Natly's grief and old despair worked like corrosive acid and Oria had to shield against it. "I can save Nolan," she said, instead of offering Natly the sympathy she'd only resent. "That's why you're here. I'm offering you the opportunity to be the agent of his salvation. What you choose to do with his trust from there is up to you. I can say, however, that once the war is done and Nolan returned to sanity and his rank, if you and he decide you'd like to be a Princess of Dru, then His Highness and I would sponsor your marriage in Arill's Temple."

Natly managed not to gape in surprise, covering it with narrow-eyed suspicion. "Why would you do that?"

"We need your help," Oria replied simply. "And you're obviously a woman of spirit and intelligence. Dru needs people like that to rebuild."

Natly considered that. Her brittle attitude relaxed a bit, and shrewd interest showed through. "What would I have to do?"

AFTER NATLY LEFT, Oria rested a moment, rallying her reserves for the next interview. Checking in with Chuffta, she asked, *"What are you doing?"*

"Flying!" he replied promptly. *"And setting things on fire! So fun. Do you want me to come get you so you can play, too?"*

"No, I have to stay here."

"Boring meetings. Burning things is way more exciting."

"You're not burning anything important, I hope?"

"Of course not." Chuffta's mind-voice had a wounded tone. *"We are not stupid Trom dragons. We're practicing precision burning while flying in formation. Lonen told us where we could practice and gave us Mikkon to teach us. Usually Mikkon works with people on horses, so he says it's a pleasure to work with such intelligent and ferocious creatures as us derkesthai."*

Oria didn't know Mikkon, but he clearly had the cleverness to flatter the derkesthai. Clever Lonen to assign him, too. *"Where is Lonen?"*

"Running around, ordering people to do things. The city is all in an uproar, people doing all kinds of things. Shall I send a small one to bring him to you?"

A "small one." Oria suppressed the laugh at Chuffta's name for derkesthai the size he'd been only weeks ago. *"No. I was just curious."*

Lonen had been up since dawn, planning to move the army out to the tunnel entrance. Oria had been up that long, too, verifying that Nolan's men were telling the truth about the tunnel's location, and clearing those stragglers who came in after the offer of clemency.

A polite knock on the door. "Your Highness? Lady Salaya is here for her summons."

"I have to go. Have fun." She sent Chuffta a mental caress of affection.

"I'd say the same, but ugh."

She had to smooth her laugh into a polite smile as Ion's widow entered the room. The tall woman looked somewhat less haggard these days. Lines of grief still bracketed her full lips, but her deep blue eyes held more interest and less angry despair. She kept her hair close-cropped in mourning, so the curls made black whorls against her lighter scalp. Without the elaborate fall of coiled hair like the others her intense eyes and arched dark brows became even more striking.

"Please make yourself comfortable," Oria said, gesturing to the chair Natly had vacated, the plates and goblet replaced, the cookie tray once again pristine. "Would you prefer tea or wine?"

"It's a bit early in the day for wine for me, Your Highness, so tea, if you please," Salaya replied with perfect politeness, but something of an edge.

Relieved not to feel obliged to drink more wine—it was early in the afternoon for her to drink, too, especially when she needed a clear head for all this mental fencing—Oria poured them both tea into finely made ceramic mugs. And because Salaya possessed far more emotional reserve than Natly, Oria opened up her senses to the other woman, seeking the source of her worries. Ah. Salaya believed she'd be run out of the palace, her sons perhaps exiled to prevent competition for the throne from Oria's future children.

"How are Mago and Kavon?" Oria inquired. "I don't believe I've seen your sons since we returned."

Salaya gave her a considering look as she stirred the sweet

syrup into her tea. "It seemed wisest to keep them out of sight," she replied baldly. "Though it was too much to hope they'd stay out of mind."

Oria shook her head. "You have no cause to be concerned for their safety. Please have no fears on that account. I can tell you now that Lonen plans to officially name Mago as his heir, should he and Arnon not return from this war."

Salaya sat back in surprise. "What of your sons and daughters, Your Highness?"

"It will be many years before any child of Lonen's and mine is old enough to be considered for the throne. If I bear children, Lonen will address the line of succession then."

"If?" Salaya raised her finely arched black brows.

Oria met Salaya's gaze with frank honesty. It would be good if they could be friends. "I don't know how well a Báran womb will accept Destrye seed. Time will tell."

A smile tugged at Salaya's mouth. "Fair warning: Destrye seed is strong stuff, and the men of Archimago's line particularly… vigilant about planting it. I have no doubt you'll find yourself with child before long."

What a wonderful thought—though they had a war to win and survive first. "If that happy day comes, I want you to know that your sons are safe, and they will always have a place in our court and our household. When we retake Bára, we'll need good rulers for that city, too, perhaps for the sister cities in time."

Salaya dipped a cookie in her tea and ate it with delicate precision, studying Oria. "Then the rumors are true. Your Highnesses are taking the armies back to Bára."

"Yes." Oria imitated her, finding the cookie even better dipped in the hot tea.

"I'm surprised you're telling me. Or that you'd consider

putting Destrye princes in positions of power in Bára."

"Your husband gave his life to end this conflict between Dru and Bára," Oria replied with solemn softness. "Your sons lost a father; you lost a husband. I lost a father, too, and brothers. Too many good people, our leaders, have perished and more will be lost still. We must treasure those we have left—and put them to good use to ensure peace and prosperity for both our peoples."

"You really believe you can take Bára, and stop them from attacking us again?"

"Yes." Oria said it with utter confidence. "Taking the city won't be easy, but I am the rightful Queen of Bára. Once the city is once again mine, I won't have to stop 'them' from attacking. We will be one people, Lonen and I will be King and Queen of a united realm."

Salaya smiled. "You don't lack for ambition, I'll say that. I accept on Mago's behalf. What else do you need from me?"

"How good are you at play-acting?" Oria asked.

HER FINAL VISITORS of the day arrived not long after Salaya left. Much as she loved the cookies, Oria gratefully accepted the platter of savory snacks her ladies brought, along with a heartier wine. She needed something with substance and they wouldn't go down for dinner for a while yet.

Baeltya and Vycayla made themselves comfortable, also helping themselves to the tapenades, nut-butters, and creamy cheeses to spread on the fresh bread. Vycayla raised a brow at the offerings. "You could've included some meats for those of us who aren't vegetarians, daughter."

Oria gazed at the platter in some dismay, as it hadn't occurred to her. "I apologize, Your Highness. My ladies have already grown so accustomed to catering to my tastes that I didn't think of it."

"Hmph," Vycayla snorted. "The Queen of Dru should think of such things when entertaining."

Baeltya rolled her eyes dramatically. "As if you *ever* entertained, Vy. Don't badger poor Oria. She's had to maneuver both Natly and Salaya into going along with this audacious plan. Successfully, too, I believe?"

Oria gave the healer a grateful smile, accepting the wine she poured. "Yes, they both agreed to their roles. Though you two will want to keep a close eye on them, regardless."

"Not me," Baeltya replied. "I'm coming with the army."

Vycayla seemed unsurprised. Oria knew Lonen had officially proclaimed that women warriors were welcome, but she didn't think Baeltya had any fighting experience. "You are?"

Baeltya nodded vigorously. "You'll need healers. I'll be leading a contingent of us. Since we can travel through the tunnels at our own pace, we should be fine."

Oria really wanted to ask if Lonen had agreed to that but thought better of it. They'd discuss it later, when they finally retired for bed. *If* they managed to keep their hands off each long enough to have that private conversation.

"You're staying here, though, Your Highness?" she asked Vycayla.

"Oh, call me Vy already as this impertinent chit does," the queen mother replied testily. "Since you won't call me 'mother.' And yes, I'm definitely staying here to keep an eye on the foxes *and* chickens. You need me to make sure you and my son have a palace to return to."

No, Oria didn't feel right calling Vycayla 'mother'—not while her own mother, Queen Rhianna might yet live. Among the many reasons Oria burned to return to Bára she longed to discover if her mother lived and, if so, what sanity remained to her. With the magic now available to her, Oria might be able to restore her mother to the woman she'd been before her husband's death broke her mind.

"We are more than grateful to be able to leave Arill City to your capable rule," Oria replied fervently, and with complete honesty. The gamble with Nolan became far less risky with the reins of actual power in the former queen's hands.

"It's my privilege and honor to defend my city and people while you're gone," Vycayla said, her gray eyes so like Lonen's bright with emotion. "When do you depart?"

Oria glanced at Baeltya, who'd just come from the war council meeting. She should've realized the healer had attended the meeting out of more than casual interest. "I've been playing tea-party politics all afternoon," she said, "so Baeltya has fresher news than I do."

"The day after tomorrow," Chuffta supplied.

"You could have told me."

"You were busy with your boring meetings." He blew a mental puff of flame at her that had the odd effect of seeming like a child sticking out their tongue. Baeltya was relaying the same information aloud.

"So soon," Vycayla murmured, reaching across the table for the carafe, pouring them all more wine. "I'm amazed Lonen can mobilize the army so quickly."

"The warriors have been on alert since we returned," Oria pointed out, "and they're almost all concentrated in Arill City or in camps between us and the tunnel entrance. We've been sending discreet messengers since we conceived this plan for the camps to begin moving in that direction, and the derkesthai have obliged in ferrying in foodstuffs that you're generously supplying." She nodded her thanks to Vycayla. "Any delay on our part plays to my brother's favor. And we don't want to risk him giving up on Nolan as a tool and sending the Trom to attack here. The sooner Natly 'frees' Nolan and he believes himself solely in power, the more likely Yar will relax into complacency."

"How soon will Natly move?" Baeltya asked.

"As soon as we're clear of the city, I'd think." Oria looked to Vycayla, who nodded agreement.

"I've got my personal guard at the temple prepared. They'll play along with Nolan as king, while making sure I'm not confined to quarters again," Vycayla said in a sour tone. "Of course, I'll have a tremendous change of heart, beg my son's forgiveness, and cater to his every whim. I hope you're right, Oria, that he'll be manageable if no longer thwarted."

Oria hoped so, too. "As soon as I can, I'll remove the geas on him. If it doesn't disperse with the death of the sorcerer who laid it on him."

"It's odd to hear you speak of these sorcerers being so easily killed," Baeltya said, mulling it over as she swirled her wine. "These terrible monsters had nearly mythic proportions to us before we met you. The stories warriors came back with…" She shuddered and gulped her wine.

"They are men like any other," Oria said. "And, like any man, they can be killed."

"And what of your last living brother, this Yar?" Vycayla asked with a sadly knowing look in her eye. "Will you be able to bring yourself to kill him?"

"If I must, yes."

"Easier to say than do," Vycayla murmured, not without

sympathy.

And yet do it, Oria would. Even if her mother begged her not to. One way or another, this last, desperate campaign would put an end to an era of conflict.

One way or another.

~ **11** ~

L ONEN WATCHED THE last of the warriors and wagon loads of supplies cross the moat, the once-teeming city almost ghostly quiet. They were leaving Arill City nearly as empty as they had on that day so long ago when Lonen accompanied his father and three brothers on a lost cause, while the caravan of non-fighting citizens departed in the other direction. This time, of course, they were leaving the city occupied with the Queen Mother in charge, but a surprisingly large number of citizens had chosen to accompany the army and fight—or assist in whatever way they could.

Those staying behind had consolidated into a tighter ring of dwellings near the palace, partly because those buildings had the best construction, and the logistics made sense—but also to create the illusion of a populated city for Nolan, and whoever might look through his eyes.

Arnon had gone ahead to organize the march through the tunnels from the lead, while Lonen—along with Alyx and three hand-picked warriors for his personal guard—brought up the rear.

Overhead, Oria rode on Chuffta, Baeltya riding behind her, the great form of the derkesthai king beside them, the sky filled with derkesthai of all sizes, flying in perfect formation. Lonen's mother stood beside him, also watching the final departure, her expression stern and expectant.

"Once you retract the moat bridge, don't extend it again for any reason until we return," he told her.

"Don't be ridiculous, boy. If people seek shelter here, of course we'll extend the bridge and let them in."

Lonen bit back a sigh. "Remember who we're dealing with here. These are sorcerers who can animate golems and who've possessed Nolan and subverted his will. It's entirely possible they could create a simulacrum of a Destrye refugee to infiltrate the city."

Vycayla's brows had climbed as he spoke, finishing in incredulous arches. "I've been dealing with the Bárans and their magic since before you were born. I'm not an idiot."

"I know." He allowed the sigh to escape. "Just… be careful. I don't like the feeling that we're leaving you undefended."

Her expression softened. "You are your father's son—but you're balancing what you can control with what you can't better than he did."

Lonen couldn't help glancing at the sky and the copper banner of Oria's hair streaming against the blue. "Nothing like a sorceress wife for lessons in what a man can't control," he commented wryly.

His mother patted his cheek, but for once the gesture felt sympathetic and not condescending. "You'll do fine." Her gaze went to the sky, too. "You two make a formidable team. Send word often, and we will, too." A small derkesthai winged over to land on her shoulder, winding its tail down her arm like a set of iridescent ivory bracelets, and Lonen was vividly reminded of Oria when he first met her. "Illya and I have worked out a system of conversation with yeses and noes, haven't we, pretty lady?"

The derkesthai dipped her chin in a clear affirmation. "I

should have done something like that with Chuffta long ago," he said admiringly.

"Yes, well, you can't be expected to think of everything," his mother replied archly, pleased with herself. "Take care of our people, and come home victorious." She embraced him, her eyes suspiciously bright, and walked off across the bridge.

Lonen took his time checking his gear, then mounting Buttercup, who had his head high and tail flicking with excitement, the warhorse recognizing the signs of battle to come. The delay let him reassure himself that the bridge had been properly withdrawn, the city and people safely within. Smoke curled up from fireplaces, hanging low in the chill air, along with the scent of meals being cooked. High above, in the towering tree Arill called Hers, the fabulous spiraling structure of Her temple perched like a beacon of peace.

Taking one last look at his home, he reflected on what it might mean that he left it for Bára a third time. A prickle of foreboding accompanied the realization, and he shook it off, Buttercup lifting his ears in question. "Nothing, man," he said quietly, patting the horse's neck. "Silly human superstitions. Let's be off," he called in a raised voice. Alyx and the others saluted, their faces full of the same eager anticipation thrumming through Buttercup.

Buttercup eagerly kicked into a fast walk, and Lonen lifted a hand to Oria, sweeping his arm forward. She waved back, and the derkesthai squadron peeled off into groups, some going ahead as the vanguard, others fanning out to scout the countryside they'd pass through on the way to Bára.

"ORIA IS READY to meet us at the first oasis," Lonen told Arnon, holding up a candle to read the message Baeltya had penned and the bright-eyed derskesthai perched nearby had brought. As soon as he read the missive, he blew out the candle, the pervasive dark of the enclosed tunnel returning.

That particular element had been left out of Nolan's stories. And—though Nolan's men had mentioned the tunnels were dark—nothing had quite prepared them for the utter lack of light so far below ground. Lonen suspected those men had been so long in the tunnels, making their way back, that they'd become accustomed to lacking sight and had forgotten.

Moving an army of warriors, support personnel, and food supplies through the tunnels without light presented various tactical issues, which Arnon muttered about pretty much non-stop. The tunnel, however, went in two directions only—forward and back—which at least made it impossible to get lost, so that worked in their favor. Other than that, they'd found themselves pressed to handle the foreign experience of being trapped underground for days on end. The Destrye were not a people who dealt with that well. It didn't help that the floor of the tunnels retained moisture, forming stinking pools in places, and soggy mud in much of the rest, slowing their progress.

Added to that, they hadn't brought along enough candles and lanterns for the entire strung-out caravan to have light all the time. They'd concentrated light at the front, in case of unforeseen obstacles, and the rest of them used light only when necessary. They'd discovered, too, that their eyes did adjust somewhat, and if they avoided light as much as possible they were able to make out general shapes of black on black.

Fortunately, the derkesthai seemed able to see just fine, so they winged their way happily up and down the tunnels, carrying written messages and bringing news from the outside world. After a week underground—and without Oria—Lonen found his own grip on reality fraying. Having the connection to her through the marriage bond kept that sun lit inside of him. He had no idea how the rest of them coped.

So, when Arnon argued—yet again—that only Lonen should go aboveground at the break in the tunnel, he shook his head vigorously, even knowing his brother couldn't see him. "Anyone who wants to go above should be able to."

"There are a lot of very good reasons not to," Arnon said, his voice muffled by whatever he was eating. "One, we could be spotted, blowing the element of surprise. Two, the oasis can't support great numbers, so not everyone can go. Three, our eyes are adapted to the depths now and anyone who goes above will simply have to adjust again."

"Four, we are not meant to live like moles belowground and I need our people in top condition."

"A desperate army fights harder," Arnon pointed out.

"Is that true?" Lonen didn't think so. "I'd rather have people remember what they're fighting for. Besides, we need to replenish the water supplies. And Oria has arranged to ferry more candles and lanterns from Arill City."

"We have a relay team to pass things along."

"Isn't it driving you crazy," Lonen demanded, "being underground for days on end like this?"

"Yes," Arnon replied evenly, not sounding anywhere near as crazed as Lonen. His hand bumped Lonen's shoulder, then gripped it. "I just keep reminding myself it's worth it. Every man and woman in this army knows that. Being upside a few hours isn't worth blowing the element of surprise."

Lonen really hated that Arnon was right. "Fine. I'll stay below and so will everyone else. But quietly pass the word among the commanders that anyone who really needs some fresh air, so much so that they'll crack without it, gets to go up."

"No, you go up." Arnon's voice held laughter. "Maybe fuck your wife and take the edge off. *You* need it."

From nearby, Alyx snickered, quickly muffling the sound. "You sound like Ion," he retorted, then regretted it immediately. Their older brother had died at Bára and had been buried there next to their father. As much of them as they could scrape together to bury.

"I think Ion would approve of what we're doing," Arnon said, and they were both silent a moment. "Does Oria have a plan for countering the Trom if the derkesthai can't stop them from landing?"

Lonen had been surprised Arnon hadn't asked it before. The looming question that haunted his own mind. They had iron weapons to fight the golems. The sorcerers they could perhaps counter with Oria's magic—though she'd be one against many. They had their own dragons to battle the ones the Trom would no doubt bring. But how to battle the Trom themselves, who seemed indestructible and could dissolve an armored warrior with a single touch?

"Yes," he said, with confidence that was a total lie. Oria would only say that she was working on it. He knew her well enough to understand that she meant she had a few ideas that she'd likely have to test in the moment, while they prayed like hell to Arill that one of them would work.

Shouts echoed from ahead, followed by flares of light, and a wave of sound as a message passed back. With the Destrye army strung out a good five leagues along the tunnel—necessary because of the space restriction and to keep the good air flowing—Lonen had appointed a person in each group to be the relay. Their one job was to accurately repeat any message they received. They couldn't afford to have messages from ahead or behind get distorted or changed.

Fenive, who'd gone with them to the derkesthai colony, served as the relay for the king's party, and she came dashing back from the next group ahead, her lantern painfully bright. Lonen closed his eyes until she shuttered it. "Golem attack at the fore," she repeated carefully and clearly, the relay from the group behind them listening carefully. "Unknown numbers."

"I'm going," Lonen said, rising and whistling for Buttercup, who saw better in the darkness than he did.

"We're with you, Your Highness," Alyx said. "Fenive, give us the light."

She took the lantern and the lead, both of them riding as fast as they dared on the uneven surface and through close quarters. Lonen gave Buttercup his head, letting the warhorse choose his footing. Forewarned, the groups of supply wagons and marching warriors crowded to the side, giving them room.

It still seemed to take forever to reach the vanguard, and it occurred to Lonen that the scouts had reported the exit to the oasis was only a few leagues beyond that. Had Oria and her derkesthai squadron landed at the oasis only to be overwhelmed by golems? The thought filled him with rage and terror. An answering pulse along the marriage bond reassured him that Oria was alive and reasonably strong. Though he knew she'd hide any distress from him.

To his great frustration, by the time they reached the vanguard those warriors had dispatched all the golems, leaving Lonen nothing to vent his fury upon. The Destrye were hacking apart the fallen, methodically chopping the pieces into bits too small to cause damage. Spotting a clawed arm, Lonen dismounted and chopped it in half with his battle-axe, a small thing, but satisfying.

"Too bad we can't eat them, Your Highness," Alby said, with a cocky grin. Lonen had put his lieutenant at the fore, trusting his former squire to recognize all manner of trouble.

"Isn't there an old saw about eating broken glass?" Lonen returned, giving the man a smile. The golems weren't made of glass, exactly, but Oria had explained that the monsters were made from the same substance as the Báran glass, but forged differently so as to be flexible, then animated. Their lethal claws, however, had a hard and sharp edge—as evidenced by the bleeding wounds on the warriors in the group. "Casualties?"

Alby sobered. "Two dead. Several severely wounded. They're with the healers."

Lonen nodded, having spotted the group working on their way past. "Were the golems looking for us—could you tell?"

"I couldn't." Alby frowned, troubled. "Do the creatures show surprise? There were an even two dozen of them, marching this way. Our derkesthai scouts saw them before they saw us. We set up an ambush and had them surrounded before they could do much."

The tunnels also made for good bottleneck fighting, thankfully turning with the landscape just enough to create ambushes at blind corners. This was the first time they'd tested it, though. A pulse came along the marriage bond, followed by a bobbing lantern. Oria came striding down the tunnel, light glowing off her copper leathers, Baeltya just behind and beside her. Both women carried swords.

Lonen glanced at Alyx. "Are the swords your doing?"

She gave him a cheeky grin. "Magic is one thing, but there's nothing like a sharp blade to boost a girl's confidence."

Oria had spotted him, slowing her headlong pace, taking in the piles of golem bodies. "You're all right?" she called.

Rather than answer, he strode to her, handed her lantern to someone else, and caught her up in a fierce kiss. He only surprised her momentarily before she kissed him back with passionate fervor. "What was that for?" she asked breathlessly when he let her come up for air.

"I missed you," he said in a low voice. "*And* I thought to keep you from embarrassing me further in front of my warriors."

Her fine, fiery brows arched in disdain. "Me, a small and simple woman, embarrassing a mighty Destrye warrior? Pfft."

"Why are you here, Oria?" he asked, still holding her close. Arill, but it felt good to touch her again.

"I felt your battle rage. And I was close, waiting for you at the oasis."

"Did you see golems there?"

"No." She frowned, extricating herself and scanning the area. "Let me take a look at these. Are any mostly intact still?"

"I'm afraid we chopped them all up, Your Highness," Alby said from a discreet distance.

"Next time leave me a torso or two," she ordered, crisp and offhand, as she knelt by a pile of the biggest pieces. It struck Lonen then how much confidence Oria had gained. With her hair bound in gleaming copper braids woven into a coronet, bound by the gleaming gold circlet of her rank, she looked queenly indeed.

Lonen signaled the others to give her room, then squatted

beside her. When they'd been attacked by golems—near this same oasis—she'd been able to absorb the packets of sgath they carried in their torsos where a human had a heart. Not a tangible thing, the sgath magic would nevertheless have been dispersed when they were chopped up with iron.

"Anything?" he asked after a while.

"I really wish I could figure out how to determine who is controlling them." Then she looked at him, the frown still on her face. "I don't like to sound an alarm unnecessarily."

"Just say it."

"I'm pretty certain they were looking for us."

~ 12 ~

"IT'S NOT LIKE reading a letter," Oria said, rephrasing the same information, yet again. "I don't get words and detailed explanations."

"Then how do you know they were looking for us?" Arnon demanded, eyes glinting blue in the flickering light.

They'd collected several lanterns and stacked them in a circle, gathering around them like it was some sort of campfire. With the mounds of still-quivering golem bits stacked along the sloping tunnel walls nearby, it made for a strange scene, even for Oria who'd at least been familiar with the golems as mindless workers in Bára. Outside of their aura of light, the blackness of the tunnel was impenetrable. Murmurs of the vast army behind them echoed uncannily off the walls, and the air sat heavy, both dank and stale.

She didn't know how Lonen had taken a week of it—though she now understood the vibrations of frustration and despair that had seeped through the marriage bond. Never mind the nightmares she woke from in a cold sweat, unable to understand why she saw Bára from the outside, the walls ever fading into the distance—until she realized they were Lonen's dreams. Ones that had abated for a while in Dru and had now apparently returned in full force.

"It's more of a feeling," she said to Arnon, who still

frowned at her. Lonen, more accustomed to magic and her inability to put some aspects into words, squeezed her hand.

"How Oria knows is irrelevant," he said, cutting off further discussion with a chop of his hand. "What's the latest from Arill City?"

"Nolan seems to believe he's king," Chuffta, listening in through her, reported via Illya. *"He crowned Natly queen and Vycayla is barricaded in the Temple of Arill, stalling him as much as possible. Salaya is pretending to be Nolan's ally and relaying information to Vycayla. But Vycayla is keeping Illya in the temple so Nolan won't see her, since you decided that seeing any derkersthai might put his watchers on alert."*

Oria repeated that for the group, then asked Chuffta aloud, "Anything on what his priorities seem to be?"

He paused a moment, and Oria heard an echo of another derkesthai relaying the question to Illya. A kind of muffled sound down another long tunnel. *"He keeps asking for Lonen and Arnon. He's been repeatedly told that they were killed in the coup that resulted in Nolan's liberation, but he demands to see the bodies."*

Lonen looked grim when she related that bit. "It wasn't enough to leave him the crown and sword. Whoever is prodding him doesn't believe we're dead. They suspect. Maybe not this, exactly, but something. So, they're sending golems to Dru, too, to assess the situation through other eyes."

"I'm afraid you're right," she said, exchanging looks with Lonen. They both knew Yar. She'd known her brother longer, of course, but Lonen had a knack for taking a person's measure quickly and thoroughly. "I think we underestimated the ability of whoever is looking through Nolan's mind. We should've gone to more trouble to make his ascension to the throne more believable."

"We took a gamble. Besides, I wasn't willing to offer my

corpse to the cause," Lonen replied with a crooked smile. "It was a delaying tactic anyway—and one intended to preserve Nolan's sanity. Had we been determined to keep all knowledge from his watchers, we would've killed him outright."

A silence fell as they processed that. Arnon shook his head sharply and stilled, mouth pressed in a grim line. "I have to say it. We can pass the message back that Nolan should be executed."

"No." Lonen's tone was resolute.

"He's a liability," Arnon persisted.

"He's also my brother who is essentially still a prisoner of war. I will not have him killed."

"He wouldn't have been so gentle with you, even before we went to Bára, and you know it."

Lonen held Arnon's gaze, gripping Oria's hand a bit tighter, then smoothing it where it rested on his knee. "I do know that—which is why I'm not going to do it."

Arnon inclined his head. "I had to argue the point."

Lonen's granite expression broke into a grin. "Yes, you did." He turned to Oria. "Will they know we killed their golems?"

She winced, thinking it through. "They'll know something did, and we might be better off assuming they know that it was here."

Lonen nodded, unperturbed by that. He'd already expected it. "So Yar knows something is up, but not exactly what. But he can at this point summon the Trom and send them to this location. It's what I would do."

"Yar is not the strategist you are," Oria pointed out.

He gave her a warm smile. "But he has advisers. I'm going to assume the worst."

"If he does send the Trom and their dragons," Arnon said,

"then we're better off in the tunnels instead of on open ground."

"Unless he floods the tunnels." Oria kicked herself for not thinking of it before. "He could. It wouldn't be difficult. You'd be trapped, along with all the Destrye, and—"

Lonen squeezed her hand hard enough to break through her panic. "We have your derkesthai scouts and messengers, remember? They'll forewarn us if that happens."

Oria relaxed fractionally, though she doubted any warning would come in time to evacuate all these people. And Lonen would no doubt insist on being the last one out. *"Could you and the Great One dig down to the tunnels in an emergency?"* she asked Chuffta privately.

"Depending on the place, yes—but there's a lot of rock on top of the tunnel in a lot of places, which would take a long time."

"It's not exactly a task worthy of one of my exalted status, sorceress," The derkesthai king boomed in her mind. ***"Fire would be faster and wouldn't get dirt in my talons."***

"Would fire burn the people inside the tunnel, though?" she asked politely, taking his cranky mind-mutter as confirmation. At least they had something of a backup plan.

"We continue as we've begun," Lonen decided. "But we increase the pace. The best way to avoid a conflict with the Trom and their dragons is not to be here when they arrive. We haven't lost all the element of surprise as they're unlikely to predict we've an entire army in their tunnels."

"We're like fish in a barrel in these tunnels," Alyx muttered.

Lonen nodded at her. "Yes, but if we take everyone aboveground, then we stand a good chance of being defeated at the oasis, far from our destination. We press forward."

"And Nolan?" Arnon asked.

Lonen glanced at Oria. "Let's end the farce. Send a message back for them to take Nolan back into custody. Not the dungeons. If they can find a way to let him believe he's still king to preserve his sanity, do it. He can be confined to quarters—windowless—and Natly may keep him company as she chooses. Vycayla can be regent for Mago, and begin teaching him what he needs to know, should he need to take the throne."

"It won't come to that, Lonen," Oria said softly, but no one acknowledged her words.

"Oria," Lonen continued, as if she hadn't spoken, "mind your scouts. If they spot the dragons before we all reach Bára, I want you and your squadron to disappear. Do not engage."

She gaped at his resolute expression, beyond shocked. "What? Why? We could fight them. That's our job."

He was shaking his head as she sputtered, keeping a firm grip on the hand she tried to yank away. "You will follow my orders, Oria, and I've made them clear: any hint of the Trom dragons and you and all of your derkesthai hightail it out of there."

"None of us will like that either," Chuffta said glumly.

"And tell Chuffta the order includes him and his," Lonen added with narrowed eyes, sensing her rebellious thoughts, if not Chuffta's actual words.

"We could harry them," she said quietly, wishing the others weren't listening so intently, so she could give Lonen a real piece of her mind. "We could be all that distracts them from going after you in the tunnels."

"No way am I spending you and the derkesthai on a delaying tactic. We'll need you at Bára to keep the Trom from landing. The Destrye can handle the city guard. We can take the walls and hold them after—but not if the Trom land."

"We won't be much use to the Destrye if you don't make it to Bára at all," she retorted.

"If the army doesn't make it there, you won't be able to take Bára without us," he replied with cool logic. "Likewise, we won't be able to take and keep the city without the derkesthai holding off the Trom. And we might as well not bother if we don't have *you* to put on the throne and neutralize Yar and his sorcerers. Either we bring all three points of attack to Bára simultaneously, or we abandon this effort."

"To do what?" she replied bitterly, unable to envision what future that might be.

"To live another day. To make a new plan. Promise me you'll obey my orders, Oria."

Her lips ached from biting down on them. "Will you walk with me a ways?"

"If you promise, here and now, before witnesses."

Oria glanced around the small circle, all of them wearing identical expressions of weary determination. Setting off on the war had been exciting, full of anticipation and hope. Now they'd settled into the part that required fortitude—and perhaps far more courage than launching the venture. "I promise to obey your orders in this," she said quietly, and Lonen relaxed his grip on her hand, stroking the back in a caress.

He pushed to his feet, giving his top commanders orders to relay down the line. A detail would be sent to the oasis to pass water down to each group as it passed that tunnel fork, but there would be no pausing. They'd accelerate to maximum pace. Then, sliding an arm around Oria and snugging her close to him, he walked her down the tunnel between segments of the vast Destrye army, alone but for Buttercup following loyally behind and the white shapes of derkesthai zipping along overhead like pale bats in the darkness.

He bent and brushed a kiss against her temple. "I'm sorry," he murmured for her ears alone.

She sighed and leaned against him. "No—you know the strategy and what you say makes sense. I just don't like being out there, knowing you're trapped down here, and I can do nothing to help you."

"Can you hold the water back with your magic, should it come to that?"

"Maybe." She resolved to practice with the oasis water, to hone those skills. "And depending on where you are, Chuffta and the Great One might be able to dig an emergency egress."

"Good thinking."

"It won't be fast enough, Lonen."

His arm tightened. "We'll have pray to Arill that they don't find us—or think of flooding the tunnel before we all get to Bára."

"I have a better idea." Turning under his arm, she faced him, wrapping her arms around his waist, needing that contact with his strong body.

He studied her face with a wary expression. "What idea?"

"Chuffta and I are going ahead, to Bára."

"Hooray! We shall save the day and everyone will write songs about us."

"Absolutely not," Lonen said at the same time, his granite command a low counterpoint to Chuffta's ecstatic warbling.

"It makes sense," she continued, as if neither of her men had spoken. "Chuffta will fly me past the bore tide flats, drop me off, and I'll enter the city by stealth."

"Wait, what? I want to go with you."

"I said no, Oria."

"I'm going to wear Tania's mask, disguise myself to look

like any other priestess, and infiltrate the city," she said, ignoring both of them.

Lonen's face set into obstinate ridges, tension vibrating through his body. "I thought you got rid of that vile thing."

"No, I simply let you think so," she replied, holding onto him when he would've pulled away from her. "We need every trick and tool at our disposal. They took my mask, Lonen, and I need one to go unnoticed. I can't take Chuffta, because he'll draw attention."

"I guess that's true," Chuffta agreed slowly.

"You'll wait nearby and help me."

"That's true! I shall fly to your rescue and they'll write songs about that.*"*

"I forbid it," Lonen said. "And you just promised, in front of witnesses, to obey my orders."

"I promised to obey you in that situation," she qualified, watching the anger flood his face, followed by resignation. "You could never stop me from doing this, Lonen. This is the city of my birth, my people, mine to deal with. I need to find my mother." Maybe kill her brother, though she wouldn't say it aloud. The superstitions of the Destrye had begun to affect her. "If I stop the sorcerer sending the golems, I can open up your path."

"We know how to destroy golems," he replied with a vicious intensity, touching a hand to his iron axe. "The Destrye figured that out long ago."

"Yes, I know, but why spend warriors on that, so far from Bára?" When he didn't have an immediate retort, she pressed on. "If I can stop Yar from summoning the Trom at all, then we won't have to fight them in the air. If I can get to him before he figures out where you are, we won't have to worry about digging you out of the tunnels before you drown."

"It would be a great joke of Arill's, to drown the Destrye as our final fate," he said, though no laughter lit his eyes.

"I don't think it would be Arill's joke," she replied very seriously. "And I have no intention of letting it be Bára's."

"Stop him from summoning the Trom…" Lonen echoed, stark realization on his face. "You mean to go right now."

"Yes. It's nighttime in the world above. I can be there and inside the walls before first light."

He set his jaw, his thoughts flying furiously through his mind as he sought an argument to stop her. "I want to forbid you from doing this."

"In point of fact, you already did forbid me, and it didn't take," she said drily.

"I don't like this." His arms tightened on her. "The last time we were separated…" He trailed off, unwilling to speak *those* words aloud.

"We came out of it triumphant," she filled in, reminding him. "Bring the Destrye to Bára, my king. The plan hasn't changed. I'll meet you there."

"You'd better," he muttered on a growl, just before he caught her mouth with his. The scrape of days-old beard contrasted with the hot, soft texture of his mouth. Arousal flooded her, nearly painful after missing his touch for a week. Her breasts tightened, swollen with need, and all her skin cried out for his, feeling stretched to bursting with neglect.

Lonen cursed against her mouth, his hands everywhere over the leathers. "I can't touch you in these things. They're a tease—showing everything and revealing nothing."

She breathed a voiceless laugh. "Just as well. We can hardly do anything with our people advancing at top speed." Indeed, the growing sound of the army on the move filled the tunnel, the section behind them rapidly approaching. "And now there's no time to dally at the oasis. It isn't the same without you."

He kissed her again, a final feel to it that she hated, even as she relished it. "I don't want this to be goodbye," he said with quiet ferocity.

"It's not." She pulled away, taking his hands in hers. "You found me in Bára twice before. Isn't the third time the magic number?"

He smiled back, though it didn't reach his eyes, which held quiet despair. His muffled thoughts echoed it, and she didn't look too closely, lest she begin to weep.

"I love you, Lonen," she said. "I'll see you at Bára."

He dragged her back into his arms, kissing her breathless. "I love you," he murmured into her ear. "I'll find you."

She knew he spoke truly. He would find her. He always had.

CHUFFTA ROSE INTO the night sky, white wings ghostly. The desert air was cool, but not as cold as in Dru. They weren't far from Bára and her hot days that lingered in the baking sands. Sgatha hung round and rosy full in the sky, Grienon sinking fast to the horizon somewhere behind them. Stars glittered thick, their light bouncing off the still oasis water below. And somewhere below that, the love of her life.

"*Lonen could've come with us. I've carried you both before, plus Baeltya,*" Chuffta pointed out.

"*I know, but we couldn't have snuck him into Bára any more easily than we could sneak you in.*" The thought of her muscled

Destrye warrior trying to pass as one of the effete Báran men had her smiling. *"And he can't abandon his people. He'll stay with them and lead them until he's the last man standing."*

"That does sound like Lonen."

And that was part and parcel of why she loved him. As much as she hated leaving him behind, they were both doing what they must, according to their natures and the responsibilities they'd been born to. She wouldn't change any of it. She could only hope that they'd triumph in the end.

A SHORT WHILE later, the towers of Bára rose against the horizon. Grienon had made his circuit around the far side of the world and rose again behind the graceful city, a blue-green jewel among the forest of towers. Though the desert sands extended all around like a lightless sea, the windows of the city gleamed with lights here and there, reminding Oria of the lovely rooms those arches and balconies connected to. Somewhere in there was her mother.

She hoped.

And somewhere in there also was Yar, and his wife Gallia, if she'd adapted to the city. Also Priestess Juli, who had waited faithfully on her, along with so many other people who'd populated her childhood. A strange sense of nostalgic familiarity warred in her heart with all the bad memories. The city seemed different now, smaller somehow. She'd seen so much more of the world since she'd fled Bára's walls. While tall and beautifully built, the towers of Bára couldn't match the forests and mountains of Dru.

She'd left this place an ignorant child at the mercy of the forces of the world, and now she returned as a queen and mighty sorceress.

"And I'm big," Chuffta chimed in with smug delight. *"Let the high priestess complain about a few songbirds now."*

Oria laughed, and the odd melancholy faded to the background. She had a job to do, two realms to serve, the populations of both counting on her whether they knew it or not. Very likely she still had a certain vulnerability to the emotional miasma of Bára, the place of her birth, and that affected her on a deep level. Mentally reviewing the balance of her magic, she adjusted her senses to allow in only what she wished for the moment, then opened her magical perception to envision Bára that way.

She gasped aloud. Gone was the lightless desert. Instead, Bára seemed to be a glittering island of magical vectors—all spinning and whirling with fabulous resonances—perched atop a sea of deep rose still magic. Bára's pool of sgath, more ancient and immense that she'd ever imagined. And the walls, the towers, most every building—all shone with blinding blue-green light. The stones of Bára were held together by grien magic, somehow held in an endlessly cycling form, drawing on the pool of sgath.

What would happen if the priestesses of Bára stopped adding to the sgath below the city? Surely those towers would fall one day, then the lower structures, the stone itself crumbling back into the sand from which it was formed. So much made sense suddenly. Of course the temple carefully taught every sorceress she could not live beyond the city walls. In truth, the city itself would not survive if her sorceresses abandoned it. Oh, it wouldn't fall immediately. Maybe not for years, but eventually the sgath would be depleted, the grien spells would fail, and it would all return to the desert.

Tucking that information away, she picked out a quiet spot, well-shadowed both magically and according to her physical vision. *"Drop me over there."* She showed Chuffta mentally. *"Then find a chasm and stay hidden until I call. You know what to do, what to look for."*

"You'll let me listen with you though, yes?" Her Familiar sounded anxious, as he so rarely did, and she sent him a soothing thought.

"Yes. And you'll be only moments away by wing. You'll know if I need you. Watch for the Trom dragons and tell me if you see them. Let me know if—when you see Lonen and the army, too."

"I know, I know. I remember. They're still on the move, fighting more golems." Chuffta set her down on the soft dunes on the moonless side of the city. Now the walls reared above her, seeming not so small at all. *"I liked being able to ride on your shoulder and miss it at times like this."*

"I miss it, too," she replied, deciding not to remind him this time that it had been his idea to be big. Unstrapping her bag and herself from his harness, she climbed down his leg, then got out the red robes she'd brought from the palace and shrugged them on over her leathers. She'd restored the priestess robes to pristine condition with her magic, and added ribbons to Tania's mask. The mask glowed with magic like the heart of a sun, and she had to make sure not to look at it directly. Fortunately, she'd discovered, once she tied on the mask, the contact with her skin dropped it out of her magical perception. It became one with her own magic, an unexpected benefit. For the moment, she left it dangling from her belt.

Reaching up to Chuffta's lowered head, she hugged his jaw, clinging to him for courage. *"Now go. Once you're away, I'll enter the city."*

"I'll be with you."

He leapt into the sky, dusting her with some sand, but not as much as he might have even a week before. He'd gotten quite skilled with flying at his new size in a short time.

His white form receded into the night, like another moon, if moons were that color. Then he vanished, and she could no longer make him out. She turned and trudged over the dunes toward the walls. It wasn't easy going, with the soft sand sliding away and dragging her down. If only she could've had Chuffta set her down closer—but that would have jeopardized them both.

She made it to the wall soon enough, though her leg muscles ached from the unusual exercise. She made her way along it to one of the smaller side gates. Putting a hand against the barrier, she extended her magical senses through it, perceiving what lay on the other side. No one was about, as she'd hoped. These side gates opened into back lots and alleys, for loading supplies, and were barricaded most of the time. The main gates would be constantly guarded, but not these sealed ones. Part and parcel of Báran arrogance, she supposed. No one without magic could open these gates, and no one with magic would be outside the city wanting in.

She untied Tania's mask from her sash, where it had dangled by the ribbons, and donned it, taking the time to weave the ribbons through her braids, tying them decoratively as if her lady's maid had done it. The metal felt warm and strangely close against her face. Eyeless, the mask made a shield against the world she found stifling after living free with Destrye.

It murmured dark things to her, but she understood it now, the way it sought to gather magic and focus it into her, and she mastered it, harnessing the artifact to do her will.

It took only a whisper of grien to undo the magically sealed locks, a bit more to clear away the sand blown against the door. She wedged it open just enough for her to slip through, then closed it again, mentally resealing the lock.

And Oria stood inside Bára, the exile returned.

~ 13 ~

I NSIDE THE WALLS, the familiar feel of home enveloped her. She'd always known—had always been told—that Bára and her sister cities had been built to create a perfect place for sgath and grien to exist in balance. Outside the walls, wild magic would erode the very life of a sorceress.

As with everything she'd been taught, those lessons contained a seed of truth, but had strayed so far from the fullness of truth as to make them into outright lies. Yes, the walls of Bára had been woven with spells that filtered out the magic of the greater world, creating an oasis of apparent peace within. With her expanded senses and understanding of magic, however, Oria understood that the sense of coherence came from homogeneity. All magic but one kind—which the Bárans and their ilk called "sgath"—had been screened out.

That process, along with the efforts of Bára's sorceress population, created the vast pool of magic beneath the city. But, like the Destrye in the tunnels for a week, accustomed to darkness and weak candlelight, then blinded by the sun, living with only one kind of magic had made the Bárans painfully sensitive to any other kind. The men in Bára, trained to draw on magic only from Bára or their sorceress companions, benefited from this system.

The women, however... They'd been made into prisoners,

captive livestock bred and trained to feed magic to the sorcerers. No wonder the men used grien so easily. They'd essentially had their magic chewed up by the walls and the women, then fed to them like milk produced by a cow.

The realization filled Oria with cold rage.

"Rage is good, as long as it stays cold," Chuffta advised. *"You're not so good at breathing fire."*

The superior tone in his mind-voice made her smile—and did help restore perspective. She was here to do a job, and she would focus on that. Time enough later, when she was recognized as Queen of Bára, to make changes, both here and in her sister cities.

So many changes she would make.

For the moment, she tucked her hands inside the wide sleeves of her crimson priestess robes and strolled out onto the smooth stones of the paved city paths. The eyeless mask prevented her from seeing the city as she had for most of her life, but her magical perception revealed far more. She understood now how wearing the mask could become a crutch for a priestess. Without the competition of physical vision, even a poorly skilled practitioner could more easily focus on only magical sight. It was hardly the badge of honor that Bárans regarded it as, however. Did a sorcerer or sorceress with real power need to advertise it via something as basic as seeing without physical vision?

The mask did give Oria the anonymity she needed, and she passed citizens and guards with serene equanimity, acknowledging their bows and greetings with a gracious incline of her head—and continuing on her important business.

Whatever a Báran priestess might be doing, it was always important.

In the same way, she strolled over Ing's Chasm and into

the palace without challenge. Yar had built a new bridge of stone over the chasm. She recognized his magic instantly, able to observe how he'd woven the stone together with his grien. If she wanted to spend the time, she could likely trace every bit of stone and sand back to where he'd pulled it from. Each bit retained a thread to where it had been before, and where and what it had been before that. Levels upon levels, strands infinitely woven together to create physical reality. Fascinating—and potentially overwhelming.

And nothing she had time for.

Especially because, as she crossed the bridge and entered the palace, the matte black taint of the Trom impacted her senses. Not present, exactly, not at that precise moment, but they'd left their essence behind, as obvious as muddy footprints on the white and gold polished marble floors. She hadn't been practiced enough when she'd encountered the Trom before to differentiate the strength of their recent presence from the more distant kind, so she couldn't pinpoint how old this trace might be.

What would she perceive now when she encountered the Trom again? She'd have to brace herself for that, because even in her formerly dulled state, they had seemed to her like black suns of magic, drawing light inward instead of radiating it. It could be they did that with all magical wavelengths, devouring everything around them.

Somehow, knowing that they'd once been as human as she—and that she carried the potential to become what they were—gave her such a chill of terror that her thoughts began to fragment. What if she became that? The peril loomed beneath her like Ing's Chasm, lightless and bottomless.

"You would never become them, if only because I won't let you," Chuffta assured her with stalwart arrogance.

"I'm holding you to that." Once again, her Familiar's steadying presence helped her regain her sense of self and perspective. She wished she could have him on her shoulder.

"It seems to me that if you were a truly great sorceress, and you made me big, you could also make me small again."

"But what if I accidentally left out important bits?" She asked in her most innocent mind-voice.

He was silent a moment. *"You're right. It's not worth the danger."*

Suppressing a giggle, feeling much lighter, she made her way to her mother's receiving rooms. When Oria was last in Bára, Queen Rhianna hadn't returned to the bedchamber she'd shared with Oria's father. After his untimely death, and how that loss tore Rhianna's mind in half, the queen hadn't been able to face their shared space. Time might have healed that wound, but Oria's instincts said otherwise. Her mother would be sleeping sitting up, staring out the window, perhaps, watching for people who'd never returned to her.

That was, if her mother still lived. Oria could help Rhianna now—show her that she hadn't lost half of herself at all—if only her mother hadn't given up. Though that would have to wait for later. For the moment, Oria had no doubt that Yar would use their mother as a hostage against Oria's good behavior. Better to secure Rhianna first, before Oria challenged Yar and took out his council.

The lack of guards posted outside the Báran Queen Mother's receiving rooms made it easier for Oria to slip inside without being noticed but boded ill for her hopes. Indeed, as Oria passed from one room to the next, she found them all unlit and still with the quiet air of disuse. She'd have to keep looking.

Oria paused a moment by her mother's chair, gazing out

the unglassed window that looked out over the city walls and beyond to the desert. A cool breeze wafted in from the distant sea, smelling of brine and moisture—and forewarning of dawn approaching. Oria had stood in that window and seen Lonen for the first time, astonished into freezing like prey at the sight of the muscled barbarian striking down the priestesses guarding the walls of Bára.

So much had happened since then, and yet here Oria stood in the same place, almost as if she'd never left.

"Who are you?" A voice asked behind her, making her whirl with a gasp of startlement as her heart skipped a beat. She should've sensed another person in the room.

A priest in golden mask and crimson robes stepped into the rosy moonlight streaming in the window. A sorcerer, who'd shielded himself from her senses. Even after all this time, she knew that voice.

"Answer my question, priestess," Yar commanded with lofty impatience. "Who are you and why are you here?" His grien snaked out, blue-green fingers to probe her, which she deflected easily. Would he notice that she did?

Why was he here in their mother's rooms and where was Yar's wife, Gallia? Oria couldn't sense the priestess anywhere nearby, but she also hadn't known her long, and the last time they'd seen each other, Gallia's sgath had been weakened by moving to a new city. Even laboring under that terrible sapping of her native magic—a sensation Oria knew all too well—Gallia had helped them to escape. Oria owed her a life, and she knew exactly how to help her if the priestess from Lousá would be willing to learn.

"Are you even a priestess?" Yar's voice climbed with offense. "It's a crime punishable by death to wear a mask not ritually given to you."

"Hello Yar," Oria said, her voice remarkably steady.

He stilled, grien tentacles of power renewing their attempt to penetrate her mind and body. To no avail, as she sent them spinning into nothing.

"Oria." Yar spoke her name like he'd found a venomous snake in the room. "How are you here? And masquerading as a priestess. I'll remind you, Oria, that's still a crime punishable by execution. But, then, you already have a death sentence on your head for being an abomination, don't you? You only escaped it because we knew you'd die outside the walls. You were supposed to die!"

How very tiresome of him. She'd forgotten over the elapsed months, in her hatred of all Yar had done to the people of Dru and Bára, and intended to do to the Destrye, what a whiny brat he was at heart.

"Where's Mother?" she asked.

"Mother is dead," Yar replied with careless insouciance. "Your fault, of course, She died of a broken heart. Knowing she'd birthed a monster, and one too cowardly to face the temple's righteous judgment, was too much for her to bear."

"Oh no," Chuffta moaned. *"Not Rhianna. We loved her."*

"We don't know it's true. Even if it is, we'll mourn later."

"She waited for you, right here." Yar's voice oozed a manufactured sorrow not even remotely reflected in his emotions. "Day after day while we searched the desert for you, only wanting to bring you home."

"Bring me home to be executed, you mean."

"It's not the fault of anyone here that you're anathema, not even our mother's. It *is* your fault that you lied to hide what you knew went against all that's good and right, and that you attempted to use that twisted, cursed, and demonic ability to steal the throne from Bára's rightful king. You may be an abomination, but your poor, abandoned mother wanted only to lay your body in the family crypt so she could mourn you properly."

"Nothing about me is an abomination," Oria replied evenly, grateful for Chuffta's mental reassurance of that, and the love flowing down the marriage bond from Lonen. It was one thing to know in her mind that she wasn't a monster, and another entirely to *feel* the truth. It took effort to resist the image Yar attempted to paint, especially when her own guilt gave it fuel. She'd abandoned her mother, the woman who'd not only given her life, but had been her greatest—and sometimes only—champion.

"But you denied her even that small peace," Yar talked over her. "She died believing you lost forever." He'd wound himself up, his wiry body tense under the priest's robes. His grien—now thick, blue-green ropes of magic, still unable to find purchase in her—flailed about her body like the tentacles of a sea creature a trader had once brought to Bára.

"Did I—or did you?" Oria retorted. "I think you, at least, knew I was alive and in Dru."

"Found my little spy, did you? I wondered." His grien stabbed at her with sudden, increased force. Enough to sting. If he figured out how she'd changed, he might be able to hurt her in truth.

Oria set all other concerns aside, studying Yar's magic. Strong, yes, but all of one flavor. And she couldn't determine whose sgath he'd filled himself with. It was all Báran sgath, processed and purified until nothing of the individual remained. Where was Gallia?

"How is it that you're alive, sweet sister?" Yar asked when she didn't reply to his accusations. She gave no sign she sensed his invasion, even as he redoubled his efforts to scan her. He was using his magic all wrong—like using a club to slice bread—but a club would smash the bread to mush. "You have no magic left at all." Yar crowed his discovery, incredulous and gloating.

"But I do. In fact, I'm more powerful than ever," Oria replied, very seriously, tempted to lecture him on drawing hasty and false conclusions. "And I can teach our people, so that we need never call on the Trom again. So that we can banish them again entirely."

Yar burst out laughing, a manic edge to it. "Silly sister. As you had little training with the temple and none with grien, you won't know that I can sense these things." His grien buffeted her once more, clumsy, but painful enough to make her scramble to convert it to another wavelength of magic.

"When I scan you, there's nothing at all," he rambled on, hitting her again, even harder. "Is that what the wild magic did instead of killing you? It stripped you of even that crippled excuse for magical potential that you never used. Now you're like your barbarian husband. Queen of the Destrye and just as mind-dead as the lot of them. You're not even a sorceress now. So that's how you lived."

Yar laughed again, grien brightening with renewed confidence. "How our parents used to go on about how you were so *special*, that your latency meant your power would bloom into something spectacular. Giving you a Familiar even. Did it occur to them to give *me* a derkesthai? No! Just for super special weakling Oria. And now it turns out they were wrong, and you have *nothing*. You *are* nothing. How utterly fitting."

"The wild magic is not what we believed, it's true," Oria replied, growing weary of his posturing. "Neither are the Trom. Their foul presence lingers here. How recently have you had contact with them?"

"What do you care? I don't even know why you're here. Could it be that mind-dead brute of a hunk of barbarian meat tired of you and dumped you back at our doorstep? If you've come crawling for forgiveness there's no tolerance for anathema in my reign." He redirected his grien, giving up on her entirely, snaking those blue-green tentacles to the stone walls around them, totally unaware that Oria could perceive exactly what he was doing. And showing her what she'd needed to see—he only reached for stone and earth. That had been his talent, but she'd wondered in the intervening months. She, herself, had an affinity for growing things, but her own magic wasn't limited to that realm. The sorcerer who'd animated the golems had died in the Battle of Bára, so someone had taken his place. She'd thought Yar, perhaps, but clearly not.

She'd have to look elsewhere—but she had to get past Yar first.

"The Trom are anathema, not me," she said, letting him hear the conviction in her voice. "According to temple teaching and our own eyes. You summoned them to attack the Destrye—broaching our treaty—and they devastated the city and Bárans along with our enemy."

"You're still stuck on that? I saved Bára! Sometimes one must cut off a limb to heal the body. Thanks to me, Bára will continue to flourish. I am the hero of this story and *you*, my mind-dead sister, are the villain." His grien fingers dug into the stones, tensing on them as a warrior might flex his muscles, giving forewarning of his intent.

Keeping a wary mental finger on the pulse of his power, Oria tried one more time. "Yar, listen to me. I've come here to help you and Bára. We are not enemies."

He paused, finally assimilating some clues. Yar had always

been bright, but too self-involved to be truly observant. "How did you get into the city anyway? This is what we've been seeing. You traitor, you brought the Destrye here. Guards—to me! We're under attack!"

And he yanked on the stones around them, chunks flying at Oria. She deflected them, sending them zooming toward Yar instead, and they slammed him to the floor. He crumpled into a heap, his grien collapsing. Had she killed him?

Stricken she moved closer to check. "Yar?"

A lightning bolt of grien shot out, striking her hard enough to stun, and she staggered back, head swirling like a sandstorm.

"Take *that*, you bitch," Yar snarled.

"ANOTHER WAVE OF golems incoming, Your Highness," Alyx reported. Even with the warmth of the light of the stubby candle she carried, the warrior woman looked wan and exhausted. They'd been battling golems nonstop, with barely a pause between assaults. In the eternal night of the tunnels, Lonen had lost all track of time. He had no idea how long it had been since Oria left for Bára.

Only the pulse of her at the distant end of the marriage bond reassured him that she yet lived. The continued waves of golems, however, bore witness to the reality that Oria had not succeeded in defeating Yar—or whoever continued to create and animate the mindless creatures. Oria was alive, yes, but in what condition?

Certainly not in any that would let her help them. At this rate, the Destrye would emerge beneath the city only to be finally and permanently decimated. At least they hadn't been drowned. Yet.

Grimly, Lonen relayed the order for a fresh battalion to move up, to relieve the group that had just spent hours chopping up the previous wave of golems. The warriors jogged past, iron weapons at the ready. Before long, another wave would pass him going the other direction, carrying the wounded back to the far end of the caravan.

"How long can we keep this up?" he asked no one in particular.

Arnon emerged from the gloom ahead, having led the previous defense and yielded to Alby for this one. All the commanders had been taking it in turns. All of them were exhausted.

"If we make the logical assumption that the golems will continue to assault us according to the established pattern," Arnon said, "then I estimate they'll chew through us in another eight assaults."

"Oh, well, is that all? We're fine then," Lonen replied, resting his battle-axe on the floor of the tunnel and leaning against the wall.

"The good news is," Arnon continued as if Lonen hadn't spoken, "I calculate that we've passed under the bore tide flats—at least the tunnels let us avoid that hazard—and if we can keep pressing forward at the same rate, we should reach the underground lake Nolan and his men fell into in fewer than three assaults."

Lonen wondered at the kind of hell they found themselves in, where they'd relinquished daylight and counted time in golem assaults. "What kind of army will we have when we get there?"

"Able-bodied warriors? About a third of what we started

out with," Alyx replied somberly.

Wonderful.

"We never planned to take Bára by might," Arnon reminded them. "We did that once before—and only because Lonen figured out how to knock their sorcerers out of action, particularly the one setting the golems on us—and we pretty near decimated our army doing that."

"I don't think bashing our heads against waves of golems counts as guile, either," Alyx commented, dabbing her fingers at a freshly bleeding slice across her cheek. "What did we plan to take Bára with again? I know we gave up on surprise."

"Stealth," Arnon supplied, gesturing at the enclosing tunnel.

"Oh right. I keep forgetting we're not actually mole people," Alyx replied wryly.

"We just need to keep ourselves in optimal form until word arrives from Oria," Lonen told them, not for the first time. "Once defeats Yar, she'll stop whoever is driving the golems at us. The city guard was always sympathetic to her rule. She'll be able to persuade at least some to open the gates."

"And if she doesn't?" Arnon demanded. "It won't do us much good to have crept here all this way if we emerge outside the city walls with the gates barred."

"She will. And, if not, we took the walls with the gates barred before. We'll just do it again," Lonen asserted.

Arnon and Alyx exchanged a speaking look. They'd developed a friendship through this campaign. It wasn't clear if their relationship was of the brothers-in-arms variety or something more intimate. Not that it mattered, but on the rare occasions Lonen found the energy, he amused himself by contemplating the latter. Unfortunately, his first impulse then was to share his speculations with Oria, which killed any lightness of heart.

"Lonen," Arnon said gently, "if Oria hasn't succeeded by now, then we have to face that—"

"She's alive," Lonen said, cutting him off.

"We believe you," Alyx supplied in the same tone. "But clearly she hasn't been able to—"

A tremor shook the earth, dirt, sand and small rocks rattling down from the tunnel roof. A bore tide, thundering above? No... something else. As if, for a moment, reality dislocated itself. The derkesthai perched on Arnon and Alyx's shoulders spread their wings, giving eerie screeching cries that had the two humans covering their ears and cringing.

"What in Arill is wrong?" Alyx shouted.

Arnon met Lonen's gaze. They both knew that feeling, had experienced it before. If Oria had been with them, she likely could have described the color of the magic wave that had just passed through.

"Nothing to do with the goddess." Arnon told her through gritted teeth, pressing his lips together as if he might puke. He remembered that day, too, when their father and brother died. "That happened before when..." He trailed off, unwilling to say the words.

"When the Trom arrived," Lonen finished for him. With renewed energy, he shouldered his axe. "Alyx, pass down the alert. Everyone who can lift a weapon to the fore. Enough of them chewing through us. We're punching through."

She saluted, mounted her horse, and galloped down the tunnel, her derkesthai messenger winging ahead to clear the way. Lonen reached for Buttercup, who stamped with delight, sensing his master's change of temperament—and the opportunity to engage in the fight at last. Thus far, they'd been forced by the tunnel dimensions to face the golems on foot.

That would change now. Shouts echoed down the tunnel, the clash of battle engaged ahead, the chants of battalions on the move from behind.

"Lonen!" Arnon said, not for the first time. "Are you mad? Even if we can 'punch through' those waves of golems, what we will we do? You can't face the Trom."

"No, but Oria can." And she'd be facing them all alone if he didn't get there in time.

Arnon kept his grip on Buttercup's cheek strap, a dangerous and bold obstinacy in the face of the warhorse's mighty impatience to be off. "Then let Oria do it," Arnon said, very reasonably, except that he shouted the words.

"We promised her," Lonen replied, leaning over to speak clearly into his brother's face. "I promised her. The Destrye army and the derkesthai squadrons must be ready when Oria signals us, to convene on the city at the same time."

"And if Oria has been taken out of the equation?" Arnon asked soberly. "Without her we can't communicate well enough with the derkesthai to coordinate strategy. Without her magic, we can't defeat the sorcerers. We learned that to our sorrow last time."

Lonen shook his head, refusing that possibility. It didn't bear thinking of—and planning around it would change nothing. "I can't control what the derkesthai will do, and I can't help Oria right now, but I *can* have the Destrye warriors where we'd said we'd be. We won't fail in this."

With that, he gave Buttercup his head. Arnon, cursing, stepped out of the way just in time. Lonen galloped at top speed down the tunnel, bent low over Buttercup's neck so his head would clear the tunnel roof atop the warhorse's towering height. His blood coursed with battle fury and he gave over control to it, letting it flow down the bond to Oria, signaling and fueling her, too.

Enough with measured progress. To hell with this waiting game. Time to engage the enemy, bust out of these cursed tunnels, and finish this war.

And pray to Arill that Oria would meet him on the other side.

~ 14 ~

"**Y**OUR HIGHNESS, WON'T you drink some juice?"

Oria stirred, blinking her eyes, her lids heavy as she opened them to see Juli—her distinctive hair curling around her gold, eyeless mask as she hovered with the proferred glass of juice—and Oria groaned mentally.

Stupid. So stupid of her to have let down her guard, not to have killed Yar when she had the chance. She could've struck him down, and she'd foolishly hesitated.

"Not foolish or stupid. You are not a predator, and he's your younger brother," Chuffta said. *"Killing isn't easy when you haven't practiced."*

"True. Thank you."

Oria sat up and took the glass, happy enough for the drink restore her wits and cleanse her dry mouth. It was her favorite kind of juice. Or, rather, it used to be. Now she understood it had been pressed from a fruit carefully nourished with the water stolen from Dru. The sweetness was a lie, covering the bitter origins.

"It's good to see you again, Juli," Oria said with great sincerity, surprising herself with the rush of emotion.

"Oh, Oria," Juli murmured, sliding her hands into her sleeves, the perfect image of calm composure that the Bárans called *hwil*. "We've missed you so. No—don't move. His

Highness King Yar unleashed his grien on you and you're gravely injured."

No, she wasn't—but how odd that Juli couldn't perceive it. Looking at the priestess she'd known for so long with her altered perceptions, Oria understood how Juli alone had been able to touch and tend Oria all those years. Juli had her magic so tightly balled up, along with her emotions, that she almost seemed to be not there, on the magical level. The priestess had become the perfect vessel they'd made her into—a funnel for sgath and nothing more—and for the first time Oria wondered what had been done to her to warp and distort her healthy self.

Feigning the injury Juli expected, Oria lay back, expanding her senses. It had only been a couple of hours, she thought, if that. Nice that Yar had summoned Juli to tend Oria, who he no doubt assumed—in his vast arrogance and the habits of a shared childhood—to be no threat. He'd even tucked her in her old tower rooms instead of a cell, falling into the old patterns of thinking she'd be days up there, recovering.

Not realizing that he'd put her in the perfect position to take over the city.

"What's going on?" she asked Chuffta, while Juli prepared one of her herbal solutions. So funny that the Bárans considered themselves the height of civilized sophistication and sorcery, but the barbarian Destrye were the ones with truly effective healing magic. One of the first things she wanted to do for Bára would be to bring a few of Arill's healers here.

"The Destrye are still fighting through the golems in the tunnels. We're waiting for them to come out," he replied promptly, though she got an impression that he was preoccupied.

"Can't you help?"

"The small ones are helping, but—"

"Would you like us to simply blow flame down the tunnel

and melt them all at once?" The derkesthai king boomed the question in her mind. *"That would be easiest, but you didn't like the idea before."*

"No, please don't." She mentally tucked her tongue in her cheek. *"I trust you both to do as you judge best."*

"Hmpf." The Great One's mental snort had a breath of flame to it. Chuffta simply sent his love and turned his attention away again. Before he did, she caught the impression of a deep chasm, a lightless lake—and hordes of golems climbing over mounds of their twitching and broken brethren. Oria sent him her love back. She sent some to Lonen, too. As always, however, he was less defined—just a burning fire of battle rage.

Alive, though. Oria shivered at the frisson of fear, despite the growing heat as the sun rose. It would be a hot day. And by the time the sun set, their futures would be decided one way or the other. Time to start recruiting allies before she went after Yar again—and finally took care of him.

"You have a fever," Juli said, approaching with the cool, soaked cloth. "Let me—" She gasped as Oria seized her wrist, shuddering in horror at the skin-to-skin contact. Yanking at Oria's grip like a trapped animal, Juli dropped the cloth, frenzied in her struggle.

Until Oria sent a calming wave through her old friend. The physical contact allowed her to loosen some of the bonds throttling Juli's free will. As with Nolan, several magical ties worked in a loop through Juli's emotions. Not libido with her, but her longing to be loved. A clever knot that tied that need for love into a need to keep her magic contained. If she wanted to love, she had to give sgath. If she wanted to be touched, she had to give sgath. If she wanted to be loved, she must keep all her sgath and give it only as the temple deemed appropriate.

Most insidious of all: Juli herself had created this spell and fed its power with her own magic.

Tempted to sever the vile circle, Oria hesitated, concerned that it might make Juli crazed like Nolan had become. Instead, she offered a suggestion, inserting an alternate idea into the loop. Juli could touch and be touched as she willed. Juli could love and be loved as she decided. Juli's sgath belonged to her, to circulate as she wished.

In her grip, Juli stilled her frantic struggles. Then she relaxed, physically and magically, like a tight flower bud suddenly unfurling into a lush blossom. "You're touching me," she breathed. "I feel…"

"You feel," Oria confirmed, then let Juli go as she got out of the bed. "There's no time for long explanations—just trust your magic. And don't believe anything they told you."

"Oria, I—what are you doing?"

Oria finished stripping off her robes. "I'm done with disguises. Where are my mother and Gallia?"

"In seclusion in the temple. A great deal has happened while you were… away."

"I'm sure," Oria replied grimly, picking up Tania's mask from the decorative tile beside her bed, the one made for that purpose. Yar hadn't taken it from her, probably hadn't even recognized its power. "They're *both* in the temple?"

"Yes. Here, I'll get new ribbons for your mask and—"

"No need." Oria tied the bits of cut ribbons to a belt loop of her fighting leathers, then strode out onto the terrace, calling over her shoulder. "We don't need to wear them, Juli. They're for focusing magic, that's all."

She gave herself a moment and no more to look around her rooftop garden, dead now, the jewelbirds fled, all the plants and trees crisped except one struggling jasmine. Even her silk shades and pillows had been left to fade and tatter in the relentless burning sun and hot desert winds, frayed bits flapping in the morning breeze. Like her old self, all of that had been lost.

Like her new self, what she built from these ruins would be better.

Resolved, she moved to the stone balustrade, fancying that her hands settled into smooth curves worn there by all the years she'd stood in exactly that spot. As she had then, she stared into the heat shimmer rising in the distance beyond the high walls of the city. No sign of violence, no telltale glitter or the shouts of warriors calling orders. Only the peaceful city, growing busier as the morning waxed on. Opening her senses to the city and its surrounds, she finally and completely used her vantage from the tallest tower in Bára. As she'd hoped, being at this height and back in this place where she'd focused so much attention on her magic magnified her perception.

Then she really and truly *saw*.

"Oria…" Juli had followed her out, sounding bewildered.

"Shh. Watch. Remove your mask, stretch out your senses, and you'll understand."

Oria didn't know if the other priestess did as she suggested or not. She cast her attention on the surging sea that was the mass consciousness of Bára. A beast of thousands of faces, hearts beating, bodies working, magic weaving. The temple taught that magic came from life itself, and Oria perceived that clearly now, how all the people, plants, and animals of Bára created the multitudes of sparks the priestesses then distilled into sgath. Without all those living beings, the city would fail— not only because no one would tend the physical aspects of people's lives, but because the magic that kept a city alive in the midst of this desert would disappear.

All those years Oria had lived on her tower, this had been what sustained and overwhelmed her. If only she'd known…

But she knew now, and that was key. Casting her mind on the surface, she dove through the currents, looking for the ones she wanted, following the scarlet, crimson, and rosy threads of priestess magic to their concentrated sources. Deep within the temple, all the priestesses had gathered with Rhianna and Gallia—in their prison cells. A part of Oria raged at the prettified term, "seclusion." Of all the sorceresses, only she and Juli weren't in that group, chanting and meditating, channeling sgath…

Ah. Channeling sgath to fuel the golem army. A small river to feed that. A larger one went to something else.

Even as Oria moved to cut off the sgath to the golems that blockaded the Destrye, another part of her mind followed the larger channel, back to a group of sorcerers. She recognized a few of them, Vico and Yar among them.

And she knew the spell they wrought.

She turned her thoughts into a blade, severing that spell, choking off the magic that fed it. Under her mental grip, it surged, bulged, and tore itself free with a clang that shook the earth, her tower swaying, and that resonated painfully on every magical level.

Juli felt to her knees, clapping her hands over her ears, as if she could block out a physical sound. Oria, her balance refined from sticking to Chuffta's back through his aerial acrobatics, rode out the waves of reaction, scanning the skies.

Boom. Boom. Boom.

One by one, the Trom dragons popped into existence, the rending of reality sending shudders through several realms. The dragons roared, their flame bright even against the sunlit sky. On their backs, the Trom riders were black motes, sucking in all light. Beneath the net of her mind, the consciousness of the city shuddered, as thousands of minds quailed in utter terror.

Too late.

"Chuffta!" she called.

"We're on our way!"

He must mean all the derkesthai. Oria whirled on Juli, who crouched on hands and knees, mask still in place. "Go find Captain Ercole. Tell him I'm here and I've brought the Destrye, that he should open the city gates to them. Then go to the temple and tell my mother and Gallia the same thing. Let them out so they can help."

"Help… what?" Juli panted, disoriented and confused. Oria pulled the priestess to her feet, using her magic to sever the ribbons of Juli's mask so it clattered to the stones. Juli cried out, clapping her hands to her face. Oria pried them away just as Chuffta landed on the terrace in a gust of wind and sand, great talons clutching the stone balustrade. Eyes wide in a pallid face that hadn't seen the sun in years, a pretty, girlish face Oria had never seen, Juli gaped at Chuffta.

"Is… Is that?"

"My Familiar, Chuffta," Oria agreed. "You remember him."

Chuffta lowered his triangular chin, giving Juli his version of a smile. *"This terrace is much smaller than it used to be."*

"No, you're much bigger." Giving Juli a little shake, she nudged her mentally, too. "Listen. I have to go turn the Trom and their dragons away from the city. Tell Gallia that I said for them to stop channeling sgath to the sorcerers. Tell her that I'm returning the favor she did me."

"But the Destrye will attack," Juli babbled.

"I am Queen of the Destrye. We're here to save Bára,"

Oria told her. She stabbed a finger at the sky. "Yar summoned the Trom because he doesn't care who he crushes to keep his grip on the city."

Juli gulped, realization dawning on her face, though hard to say if it would be enough. "What if the Trom land? Their least touch is death."

"No, it's *not*." Deliberately, Oria laid a hand on Juli's pale cheek. "Could I do this before? That's right." She nodded at Juli's widening gaze, her brown eyes that Oria had never seen so pretty with their tawny flecks. "I can control the touch now. That's all the Trom do. They're just like us, with a different magic. Control what happens if they try to touch you."

"I don't understand," Juli nearly wailed.

"Trust me. You know me. Release the others. Stop feeding the sorcerers sgath. The Destrye are here to help. Let them. As soon as I can, I'll join you at the temple." Impulsively, she kissed Juli's cheek, and released her.

"*Let's go.*" With a running start, Oria leapt onto Chuffta's leg and climbed up the rope harness she quickly wove onto him from her dead garden.

"Oria!" Juli called, face stark with uncertainty.

"If you love Bára, do as I ask. Go set the priestesses free. Use your magic. Use it for Bára."

Another dragon swooped over them and Oria ducked reflexively, then saw it was also white. The derkesthai king, with a rider on his back... Baeltya. The healer waved, then pointed at the sky. Chuffta leapt into the air to follow, the derkesthai of all sizes massing behind them in their patterns, turning the sky as white as if the snows of Dru had come to Bára.

They surged up in formation, ready to engage in battle.

"*Anything from the Destrye?*" she asked, reinforcing her

straps and gathering the rivers of magic from her home city and the wild magic beyond.

"They are closer, but not yet through. Maybe Juli will get the others to stop Yar and whoever is sending the golems."

Maybe. Torn, Oria cast about again for that river of magic feeding the golems, but the presence of the Trom had disrupted everything. Instead of a living sea, the magic of the city jumbled in chaos, the streams of it warping and bending around the infinite deep holes that were the Trom.

"She'll have to. Let's go knock these monsters out of the sky."

~ 15 ~

L ONEN SWUNG HIS iron axe with grim determination, ignoring the sweat dripping from his soaked hair into his eyes. The three golems charging him dropped with the single blow—and four more took their place. Emotionless, thoughtless, the monster creatures advanced in relentless, silent waves, tearing with long, saber-sharp claws, rending his flesh with crystalline-fanged mouths if they got near enough.

Far too often, the mindless creatures got near enough, and Lonen knew he'd grown as slick with his own blood as sweat, though he felt none of the wounds. The tunnel had widened as it approached the lake and chasm, and Buttercup waded in water up to his hocks at times. That meant the other warriors, like Alyx at his off side, were in up to their thighs. It made the endless advance that much more grueling.

At least they had light. Not direct sunlight, but daylight filtering down from somewhere ahead. They were so close.

Any moment now, Oria would stop the sorcerer animating these things, and they would fall into motionless heaps. He fantasized it so clearly he sometimes thought—in the nonstop fugue of killing—that it had happened already.

But no.

No, the golems kept coming and coming.

If Oria was alive—he knew she was alive. He could feel

her, couldn't he? Sometimes he wasn't sure he felt anything but the strain of his muscles, the pumping of his heart, the endless sweep, chop, advance, sweep, chop—but if Oria was alive, she'd stop the golems. Any moment now they'd fall into motionless heaps.

How many of Arnon's assault waves had this been? Probably the metric had fallen apart with Lonen's decision to make a hard push. No doubt Arnon could chart it, how the force of the Destrye army disrupted the regular waves of golem assaults, compressing them into one unending mass, like life in the tunnels, like the passage of time, squeezed into agonizingly slow progress...

A shout from ahead. Then a roar of dragons, echoing from high above. Lonen renewed his vigorous swinging, mowing down the golems like the farmers did the ripened stalks of grain. If only he could feed his people from fallen golem parts.

And then... the golems collapsed. Just as he'd imagined countless times in the last exhausting hours. They simply froze mid-movement, then crumpled, bobbing up again to float away like soap bubbles and catch in eddies. Oria had done it!

Buttercup lifted his head, trumpeting a challenge, and charged forward, sending golem bodies surging away on the waves. The Destrye roared also, in one voice, a wave of warriors brandishing weapons as they sought the daylight.

As promised, the derkesthai had been busy while they waited, tumbling rock and tamping the dirt into a ramp leading out of the chasm. Lonen and Buttercup galloped to lead the vanguard, his captains on their warhorses raising flags to gather their contingents.

They rode up and out of the tunnels, rising through the crack of the chasm into full day. Above, a fierce battle rumbled and thundered through the sky like the summer storms of

Lonen's boyhood. Green flame crackled like lightning, and the dragons and derkesthai roared with earth-rattling challenges.

Trusting to Buttercup, Lonen studied the two biggest white dragons. Chuffta and the Great One, especially from this distance, looked much the same. Both bore a rider. He couldn't make out which was which. Though both seemed locked in lethal battles of aerial acrobatics and flame that seemed certain to end in disaster.

"Lonen!" Arnon rode up hard on his flank. "The gates aren't open."

Lonen wrenched his gaze from the sky and focused on the ground. His job was to get the Destrye in the gates to secure Bára. "Then we'll open them."

Setting up the signal, he turned his army to once again—and for the final time—take the city of Bára.

At Chuffta's mental alert, Oria seized a moment to look down. The Destrye poured up out of the chasm outside the walls of Bára like ants swarming a fallen beast. The city, however, wasn't prone. The towers stood tall and graceful, remote behind her walls, proudly peaceful—and with gates firmly shut, no sign of activity within, turning a deliberate blind eye to the battle raging outside.

The Báran way of dealing with everything, apparently. But that would change.

As Chuffta dipped in a deep sideways tilt to come about, Oria spotted Lonen, easily distinguishable by Buttercup's black bulk. The warhorse climbed a small outcropping with ease, and Lonen looked to be shouting orders, using his massive double-headed, battle-axe to point the way. Her heart eased. She'd known he lived, via the marriage bond and the reports of the derkesthai, but seeing him hale and vital reassured her on another level. She could swear he looked up just then, the arrow of his distant gaze slamming into her, and the bond between them thrummed. Smiling, she pumped a fist, though she knew he likely couldn't see her well.

"Duck!" Chuffta's mental shout came at the same moment he folded wings and dove, a roar of green flame singeing overhead and heating the already crackling air. The dragon dove after them, the Trom on its back briefly parallel to her as Chuffta pulled up again to avoid hitting ground.

It sat astride its mount with no apparent apparatus to keep it there, clinging like spiders can to any surface with ease. And it stared right at her. Calm and without expression on its smooth face, it gazed at her as if they'd met in an elegant salon instead of plunging through the air on flaming dragons. The matte black eyes dominated its spherical skull, draining away the visible light as well as all the magic around them. Oria considered hitting it with her magic, but instinct stopped her.

"Careful." The Great One blazed fire at another Trom and its dragon, herding them away from the city. ***"You might not be able to detach again."***

The last thing she wanted was to create a connection to that monster, one that might doom her to be leashed to it forever if she couldn't break away again.

For the first time, however, she saw for herself what the derkesthai king had told her: how the Trom looked like her own people, slim and long limbed, with fine bones. The way its skin clung to its skeleton made the Trom seem so alien and insectile, but in that face, those pits of eyes… Oria glimpsed the sorcerer it had once been.

Or sorceress.

Chuffta peeled off, ending the moment as he evaded a crash, and Oria—caught momentarily unware, reached for the straps to steady herself, hand brushing Tania's mask as she did. The thing nearly burned her, so hot and bright.

Images flooded her—of Bára, recognizable, but different. A Bára with no walls, perched on a great river, with trees! Feathery branches flowering, the lovely trees arched over the placid water, creating cool shade. In those memories, Oria knew how that shade felt, the deliciously refreshing feel of the water. And overlaying all of it, magic—wild and tamed—weaving and flowing together in balance and harmonious life.

Then a patchwork rush of images: A new moon appearing in the sky, bright blue-green that whirled madly past every few hours. The sun burning hot in a cloudless sky. The river becoming smaller, the trees wilting, then crisping. Desperate efforts to manipulate magic, to affect the weather itself. The walls rising around Bára as the riverbed became desert.

The mask. Oria had named it for her aunt Tania, a woman she'd never known, as the ancient sorceress who'd been buried with the mask hadn't had a name inscribed on her tomb.

So powerful. So ambitious and determined, Oria's mother had told her long ago, before she fled Bára. *Don't be like her, Oria. Find an ideal husband and channel your magic through him. Don't try to do it alone. Don't be like Tania. Promise me.*

But Oria didn't have the ideal husband they'd intended for her. She channeled her own magic—and she wasn't alone.

She reached out with her magic and connected to that Trom.

"Oria!"

"I know what I'm doing." She hoped. The Trom didn't fight

her grip, but slithered back up it, filling Oria's magic portals with oily slick darkness. *"Land us inside the walls."*

"Them too?" Chuffta's mind-voice sounded bewildered. *"Ugh! I can taste it through you."* He made mental gagging noises.

"Them too." Concentrating, Oria held firm, resisting the visceral urge to drop the connection, and trying to filter it at the same time, to spare Chuffta. *"Take us to the temple court-yard."*

"But the whole strategy was to keep the Trom out of Bára," Chuffta complained, even as he angled them into a steep glide, heading for the expanse of plaza between the palace and temple.

"I'm changing the strategy," she replied tersely, most of her concentration going to coercing the Trom, who'd begun to tug in the opposite direction. Not to break free—no, its claws sunk ever deeper into Oria's psyche—but to pull her away from Bára and its walls. Which only confirmed to Oria that she had the right idea. *"Tell the Great One to keep all the others away still,"* she added, finding it easier to speak along the time-worn channels between her and her Familiar.

She felt the pang of concern from Lonen as he observed their descent, and sent him a pulse of reassurance, hoping he'd understand. Then she had no mental space for anything but hanging on to the Trom as they crossed the walls, the magic disruption of them like a bore tide crashing through her consciousness, and then again crossing Ing's chasm. She dragged the Trom with her, forcing its dragon to land.

Golden masked priests and priestesses spilled out of the temple, but Oria focused on containing the dragon, holding its mind along with her connection to the Trom. As soon as Chuffta landed, Oria scrambled down the harness straps, pulling the Trom now opposite her on the stone apron to do likewise. It followed suit, moving with spidery ease, as if Oria weren't compelling it. In truth, Oria couldn't tell if she really was making it obey or if she'd fallen into its web.

"Keep that dragon contained," she told Chuffta.

"On it."

As Oria and the Trom walked toward each other, facing off, she saw Chuffta backing the Trom's dragon to the edge of the precipice. The darker dragon tossed its head but retreated before the much larger Chuffta and his well-placed flame. The priests and priestesses shouted, incomprehensible, male and female voices combined—and Oria spared them no attention.

Every fiber of her awareness focused on the Trom.

"Ponen no longer, I perceive," it rasped in its hoarse voice, as devoid of melody as its frame was of human flesh. "You are one of us now."

"No," Oria replied evenly. "I'm what you could've been, ancestress, had you not lost your way."

Its lipless mouth smiled without mirth. "There are ways and ways, child, and you will find that everything dries up and dies but one thing: power."

"You're wrong." Oria untied the mask from her belt and held it out to the Trom. "I believe this was once yours."

The Trom extended its bare twig fingers. Not unnaturally long, but a once-human hand stripped to skin, ligament, and bone. Without the fleshy palm, the finger bones extended from the knobby wrists, creating an illusion of length. The Trom took the mask and held it, staring down at the shining artifact, arrested. "Not mine," it said. "But one I once knew."

A hint of wistfulness came from the Trom, the first taste of emotion Oria'd had from one of them. "A long time ago," Oria suggested.

The Trom raised its unearthly gaze back to hers. "Longer than you can imagine."

"Longer than anyone should live."

"Who's to decide such things? Some things fade too fast, are gone in a blink. Others last far too long, wearing us down to nothing. We did what we had to do not to die."

"The world changed when Grienon arrived," Oria ventured. "You used magic to keep yourselves alive, then couldn't die."

The Trom inclined its head. "You would do the same."

Oria shook her head. "There are other ways."

"Now there might be, but only because of us."

"That could be," Oria allowed. "But you are not harnessed to us. You do not have to answer the call of Bára any longer. Our battles are not yours."

The Trom turned its head, raising the hand not holding the mask and beckoning to someone with an uncanny undulation of those spidery fingers. As if released from a stranglehold—perhaps he had been—Yar barreled forward, shouting imprecations.

As one, Oria and the Trom regarded his frothing posturing with bemusement. "This one summoned us," the Trom informed Oria, a whisper of dry humor in it. "And you say we do not have to answer? The magic compels us. We do not like it."

"If I promise to break your chains," Oria spoke over Yar's impotent yelling, "will you call off your brethren above?"

"You believe you can?"

"Kill her!" Yar shouted, seizing Oria by the arm in a painful grip and shaking her. "I am the Summoner and I command you to kill her."

"I can," Oria replied to the Trom, ignoring Yar. His grien

batted at her, but she held him off.

"Prove it," the Trom said, holding out its hand. "Touch me. If I don't kill you, I'll believe."

Watching the Trom's magic, seeing how the currents of it pulsed to suck all life from whatever it touched, Oria changed her own to both match and deflect. She laid her hand in the Trom's, clasping it in what felt like the beginning of a very strange friendship.

The Trom smiled. "Perhaps you can. But you must kill the Summoner."

Everything in Oria congealed, going cold and dense. "He is my baby brother."

Cocking its head with what might be sympathy, the Trom squeezed her hand and released it. "I know. And I've shown you how. Break our chains now. Kill the Summoner, and we'll go. I'll trust you to make sure we can't be Summoned again."

Yar still had her arm, attacking her with his grien. It felt much weaker now, and Oria became aware that one group stood well back, their sgath still and contained. The priestesses, refusing to feed the priests.

Three women stepped to the fore, hands clasped and faces bare. Juli on one side, the golden-haired Gallia on the other, and Oria's mother, tall and straight in the middle. The queen mother observed her two surviving children with a careworn expression, but a sharp, alert gaze. She met Oria's eyes and dipped her chin.

With a deep sense of regret and righteousness, a conflict Oria knew she'd spend the rest of her life resolving, she turned in Yar's grip and embraced him. Letting the black current reverse, she pulled his life force into herself, feeling him dissolve into nothing, and collapse in a pile at her feet.

~ 16 ~

LONEN HAD FORGOTTEN how high those walls around Bára reared up, the towers dizzyingly tall beyond that. Difficult to believe he'd once scaled that impervious reach. Though he had done it—and had climbed trees far taller. The wall only seemed unscalable now because Oria was behind it, facing one of the lethal Trom.

Buttercup valiantly galloped through the sucking sands at a diagonal from the rock outcropping they'd stopped at after climbing out of the chasm. They made for the trade road, the Destsrye army whooping and shouting in fine aggressive barbarian style behind them. Oria would be amused by it, and Lonen clung to that image of her—alive and laughing, not in a gelatinous pile. He let the feel of her burning sun at the other end of the marriage bond draw him closer, though the gates to the city remained firmly shut.

If he had to climb those walls again, he would.

With a clatter, Buttercup's hooves found the hard-packed road, and he put on a burst of speed, heading for those unmoving gates. Overhead, the dragons battled with guttural roars and blasts of flame.

Then suddenly, the skies went silent.

Responding to Lonen, Buttercup reared up, wheeling in a circle to lash out at whatever had changed. But only white derkesthai remained above. The Trom and their dragons had disappeared.

With a shout, Lonen turned Buttercup and the army back toward the gates, resuming their headlong approach. Hardly daring to hope they might have won, Lonen thought as hard as he could at Oria, praying to Arill that she could hear him.

And the gates opened. The city guard of Bára poured out, lining either side of the gates, raising swords… and then laying them down. Without pause, Lonen and Buttercup galloped full speed through the tunnel in the wall, a space Lonen remembered all too well from long hours taking and holding it against the city guard.

As they emerged from the shadows, the enormous white figure that was Chuffta landed in the wide courtyard. On his back Oria perched, copper hair streaming wildly from her aerial battles, a broad grin on her face.

They both leapt from their mounts and ran, catching each other up in a hard embrace. Her light, lithe body vibrated against him, thrumming with magic and victory. He kissed her, hot and long, savoring the flavor of his sorceress queen.

When they parted, both out of breath, he gave her a cocky grin. "The last time you surrendered Bára to me, you rode a white horse instead of a white dragon. It seems you've come up in the world."

"Well, it's important to dazzle the barbarian hordes at your gates," she replied with a saucy smile.

"Where do we stand?" he asked, sobering.

"Yar is dead." She grew somber, too, haunted shadows in her copper eyes. "I killed him. Lonen—I used the Trom power to do it. I dissolved him while I held him in my arms."

He gazed back at her, letting her see and feel the love and regard he held for her. "You used the tools at hand, Oria, to do what you had to as queen of two realms. You restored the balance, yes?"

Her eyes filled with tears. "I hope so," she whispered.

"You did." He gave her all his confidence in that truth. "And now we move forward. The Trom?"

"Gone," she answered. "That's a story."

"All right then." He let her go and found Arnon and Alyx standing nearby. From behind Oria, a group of three women riding horses and dressed in priestess robes, but not wearing masks, approached. "I suppose we have a great deal to sort out."

"Yes." Oria sighed, sagging briefly against him, then straightened. "The city council and temple are in complete disarray, but let me introduce you to women you've met, but may not recognize. You'll remember my mother, Rhianna."

The tallest woman, with the look of Oria, dismounted and came toward him. Remembering the epithets the queen mother had hurled at him before, Lonen gave her a cautious bow. "Queen Rhianna," he said, straightening, then putting an arm around Oria to draw her to his side. "It's a pleasure to see you alive and well."

She gave him a severe look, noting his possessive gesture. "How gratifying. I offer you two things: my apology for what I said about your suitability as a husband for my daughter, and my thanks, for saving her life. Your Highness," she added with a wry twist of a smile that reminded him oddly of his own mother.

He looked down at Oria, who had her face tilted up to his, an echo of the same amusement in her smile. "Oria saved herself," he said, as much to her as to Rhianna. "And Bára, it seems."

"Because I have the ideal husband," she teased. "And this is

Juli, without her mask."

The pretty young woman with tousled red curls gave him a smile and a bow. "Your Highness. Good to see you returned to our walls."

Lonen grinned back at his one-time co-conspirator in handling his then new and skittish foreign bride.

"And this is Gallia," Oria said, drawing forward the elegant blonde. "You encountered her briefly at the duel that had me excommunicated from Bára. We have her to thank for so much, including saving my mother's sanity."

"That's putting it strongly," Gallia demurred, staying a careful step back from Lonen and casting her gaze downward. Remembering how Oria had said his presence affected her before she learned to manage it, Lonen made an effort to pull his thoughts and curiosity back. Oria stroked a hand over his forearm in appreciation.

"It's not." Rhianna gave her daughter-in-law a fond look. "Gallia took Oria's advice and sought out my friendship. She sat with me daily, helping me come out of a very dark place."

"You helped me through my dark place," Gallia returned. "Leaving Lousá weakened me in ways that I never expected— or could've dealt with on my own. That and being married to Yar—" She cut herself off, looking anxiously between Oria and her mother.

"Yar nearly killed Gallia," the queen mother said baldly. "He drained her dry, trying to force her to adapt to Bára's sgath. "He was… not kind to her. Something I shall bear the guilt for to my dying day."

"His actions were not yours," Gallia countered. "You're not responsible."

"I am." Rhianna nodded to herself. "I raised that boy to be who he became. I mourn my son's death, but I don't regret the necessity of it. I'm only glad I had the wit to raise a daughter like Oria, too." She opened her arms and Oria ran to her, the tears falling freely now. They rocked each other for a long moment, then Oria stepped back, holding out a hand to Lonen, drawing him into their group.

"Juli rallied the priestesses to cut off the flow of sgath to the priests," Oria explained to him, wiping away her happy tears. "Gallia had been gradually draining Yar already. They were able to cut off the flow to the golem army."

"And Nolan?" he asked. "Yar or one of his priests had a magic hold on my brother. Is it gone or is it too soon to know?"

Oria glanced at Gallia, who considered. "We cut off everything. There should be no grien leaving Bára now."

Oria's eyes took on that abstracted look she got when speaking to Chuffta mind-to-mind. "Chuffta asked Illya, the derkesthai with Lonen's mother," Oria explained, for everyone's benefit. "The spell binding Nolan seems to have snapped when that sorcerer was cut off from Bára's sgath. He's disoriented—he remembers very little of what occurred since he fell into the chasm on the battlefield here—but seems to be more himself."

Her face echoed the relief Lonen felt, as that scar of guilt and worry unknotted itself. Behind him, Arnon and Alyx spoke to each other quietly, sounding equally pleased.

"How do you have so many derkesthai?" Rhianna asked her daughter, then cocked her head to eye Chuffta askance. "Is that really Chuffta?"

Chuffta lowered his great head to rest his pointed chin on the ground, blinking his bright green eyes at Rhianna fondly.

Oria laughed. "Yes. I used my magic to make him big."

"Apparently," Rhianna replied faintly, still raptly staring.

"Thank you for him, Mother." Oria became very serious. "I don't know how you knew I'd need him, but I did."

Rhianna looked back at her daughter. "My sister Tania told me to get him when you were born, before she left Bára. She recognized in you what our great-grandmother had. Tania had special insight that way, an admirable skill."

"But you told me not to be like her," Oria exclaimed.

Her mother sighed, looking to Lonen. "I wanted my life for you, and for Tania, and that was selfish. I think you're both better off having followed your own paths. At least I hope so in her case, wherever she may be."

Gallia cleared her throat. "Speaking of having cut off all of the priests' grien, we'll need to remedy that soon, or vital spells like those powering the walls and the orchards will collapse."

"We'll have to determine which priests can be trusted," Rhianna put in gravely.

"You can learn to do it yourselves," Oria corrected decisively. "I'll teach you. The trustworthy sorcerers can learn to filter the wild magic—and so can you—and the sorceresses can learn to wield active magic."

"But women can't use grien," Juli blurted, then looked chagrined at Oria's laugh.

"There is no such thing as sgath or grien," Oria corrected gently, not without compassion. "Those are constructs, created long ago to bind us to our roles. We don't need them any more than we need the masks. In time, even the walls can come down. The time we needed that barrier to protect us has passed."

"Including protection from the Destrye," Lonen added. He glanced behind him to see Alyx and Arnon, exhausted and covered in blood and other nameless substances, but grinning with hope. Beyond them, the Destrye warriors mingled with

Bára's city guard, some in conversation, renewing acquaintances from the time the Destrye had occupied the city in peace. He squeezed Oria's hand. "We are one people now."

"Which means I'd like Arnon—" Oria looked to Lonen's brother, who stepped forward with a bow. "Arnon, can you set up a system to start ferrying food and water through the tunnels back to Dru?"

"Of course, Your Highness. I look forward to the challenge."

"We're sending food and water to Dru?" Rhianna asked, eyebrows climbing in her pale face.

"It's about time Bára began making up for all it's stolen from Dru over the years, don't you think, Mother?"

Rhianna opened her mouth, gaze sharp, then closed it again. She nodded in resignation. "Perhaps so. But don't strip us bare, I beg you." She said it to Lonen, but Oria answered.

"There is no more us and them." Oria looked up at him with an affectionate smile. "Teamwork, yes?"

"Absolutely," he agreed. "And we'd best get to it. There's a great deal of work to do."

"True, but…" Oria's smile turned flirtatious. "You're awfully filthy, barbarian. As Queen of Bára, I'm commanding you to bathe and make yourself fit for my presence."

"Is that so?" he murmured, remembering Bára's luxurious baths and the fantasies he'd nurtured about Oria in them the last time she'd issued that command. "Maybe I'll toss you over my shoulder and carry you there."

Her eyes sparkled with laughter, and she rose up on tiptoes to reply in his ear. "I do recall promising *total* surrender, once upon a time."

"And thus the conquered becomes the conqueror," he replied, turning his head to capture her mouth with his.

Heedless of all watching them, Báran and Destrye alike, Oria and Lonen kissed, celebrating a lasting peace and partnership. And all around them, people and derkesthai cheered.

~ Epilogue ~

ORIA AWOKE, ALONE in the bed and with late morning sun streaming in. She stretched, muffling a groan, her body heavy and sluggish. Even though she'd clearly outslept Lonen, she felt like she could sleep for days more.

"Sleep as many days as you like," Chuffta suggested. But his bright green eye appeared in the window, blocking the sunlight. *"How are you feeling?"*

"Eleven months pregnant, thank you."

She rolled to her side and used her hands to push herself up, the way Baeltya had taught her. *"It's much better our way,"* Chuffta commented, watching her. *"Lay the eggs and wait for them to hatch instead of carrying them around inside you."*

"I'll keep that in mind for next time." As a first order of business, she relieved her poor, crushed bladder, then pulled on a robe and opened the glass-paned doors to step out onto the rooftop terrace. The autumn sun filtered through the fiery canopy, the surrounding forest a spectacular display of color. Chuffta lolled on his platform nearby, soaking in the sun, the tip of his tail flicking in lazy delight. The planters surrounding the terrace overflowed with flowers, vines, and even small trees and bushes. As the Destrye had ventured out of Arill City over the course of the summer, reclaiming lost homesteads and discovering new ones, they'd vied with each other to bring

back anything that flowered that their queen might not already have in her garden on the roof of the palace.

Combined with the plants from her Báran garden, coaxed to verdant life from seed and shoot, the array made for an exotic bouquet unlike anything else in the world. Arnon had surprised her with the once-dying jasmine tree from her tower garden in Bára, having it brought through the tunnels along with food supplies, calling it a belated wedding gift. Songbirds from all over—even a few hardy jewelbirds—gathered in the branches or flitted from flower to flower. The flora and fauna of Bára and Dru complimented each other with a surprising amount of balance and symmetry. A sorceress's garden sustained by her magic and careful attention.

Arill knew she didn't have the energy for much else.

"She's awake," Lonen called out, coming through the doors she'd left open.

She opened her arms and he gathered her close, carefully maneuvering around her distended belly, kissing her thoroughly. "I was worried you'd sleep through lunch," he teased.

"I already missed breakfast, apparently," she replied with a smile. "I'm starving."

"Good thing I'm king then, because I have ordered a feast fit for a queen." A queue of servants streamed out the doors, carrying platters of food they arranged on the table set in a pool of warm sun.

"How many people are you planning to feed?" Oria asked, raising her brows and laughing.

"At least three," Lonen answered, laying a big hand on her belly. "You, me, and this one. What's your guess today— barbarian warrior or sorceress?"

"Could be warrior woman or sorcerer," she reminded him.

"Copper hair, though."

"And gray eyes. A handsome combination."

"Maybe he'll be a mighty thewed sorcerer," Lonen suggested with a sparkle in his own gray eyes as he helped her into a chair.

"Or she will be," Oria retorted, giggling at the expression on her husband's face. She took his hand. "No matter who our children are, magically gifted or not, mighty warriors or not, we'll love them and teach them."

"Just so long as they aren't annoyingly over-analytical engineers like Arnon," Lonen mock scowled. "I can't love that."

"I heard that," Arnon said, strolling out from inside, Alyx with him, smiling warmly at Oria.

"This is a private lunch," Lonen pointed out. "And the royal couple's private quarters, need I remind you."

"Good thing the queen has a soft spot for me." Arnon gave Alyx a nudge with his elbow, and Oria a jaunty wink. "We received a message from Nolan. He and Natly have settled in at Lousá and are making headway with diplomatic relations."

"Helped along, no doubt, by the promises of wood and water from Dru," Lonen commented cynically.

"In exchange for for what they can send us," Oria reminded him. "It balances out, and we're all benefitting from working together instead of warring."

"I know, I know." Lonen pretended to scowl. "Hopefully we won't get bored with all this peace and prosperity."

"I'm sure something will come up for you to bravely battle," she soothed.

"In the meanwhile," Arnon said, and presented her with a sheaf of scrolls and a gallant bow.

"Ooh, thank you, Arnon!" Eagerly, Oria unrolled them, scanning the designs with an eye grown considerably more practiced.

"Dare I ask what those are for?" Lonen canted his head to look.

"Addition to our apartments," Oria said, handing him one. "The baby will need a room with access for their derkesthai Familiar."

Lonen grunted, studying it. "Surely not yet."

"Which?" Alyx quipped, giving Oria's belly a jaundiced eye. "The baby or the Familiar, because to my unpracticed eye, our queen looks ready to pop."

"Ugh," Oria replied, rubbing a hand over the uncomfortably stretching skin of her belly. I feel like could. But I meant the Familiar. I want to incorporate our child's room into the framework for the greenhouse, which I need in place before the first frost." And hopefully before she had the baby.

"Greenhouse?" Lonen echoed.

"Yes," Arnon replied with enthusiasm, waving his hands at the rooftop garden. "I'm framing in all of this and Oria will conjure the glass."

"That way the plants will survive the winter," Oria explained. "Come spring, I'll remove the glass again."

"Handy," Lonen commented in a dry tone.

"Yes." Oria gave him her sweetest smile. "I am. And you promised to give me whatever I needed to make me happy here in Dru."

He lifted her hand and kissed the back of it, gray eyes glowing with love. "And have I?"

"Always and forever," she answered.

TITLES BY JEFFE KENNEDY

<u>FANTASY ROMANCES</u>

BONDS OF MAGIC
Dark Wizard
Bright Familiar
Grey Magic
Familiar Winter Magic (In Fire of the Frost)

HEIRS OF MAGIC
The Long Night of the Crystalline Moon
(also available in *Under a Winter Sky*)
The Golden Gryphon and the Bear Prince
The Sorceress Queen and the Pirate Rogue
The Dragon's Daughter and the Winter Mage
The Storm Princess and the Raven King (May 2022)

THE FORGOTTEN EMPIRES
The Orchid Throne
The Fiery Crown
The Promised Queen

THE TWELVE KINGDOMS
Negotiation

The Mark of the Tala
The Tears of the Rose
The Talon of the Hawk
Heart's Blood
The Crown of the Queen

THE UNCHARTED REALMS
The Pages of the Mind
The Edge of the Blade
The Snows of Windroven
The Shift of the Tide
The Arrows of the Heart
The Dragons of Summer
The Fate of the Tala
The Lost Princess Returns

THE CHRONICLES OF DASNARIA
Prisoner of the Crown
Exile of the Seas
Warrior of the World

SORCEROUS MOONS
Lonen's War
Oria's Gambit
The Tides of Bára
The Forests of Dru
Oria's Enchantment
Lonen's Reign

A COVENANT OF THORNS
Rogue's Pawn
Rogue's Possession
Rogue's Paradise

BLOOD CURRENCY
Blood Currency

<u>BDSM FAIRYTALE ROMANCE</u>

Petals and Thorns

Thank you for reading!

ABOUT JEFFE KENNEDY

Jeffe Kennedy is a multi-award-winning and best-selling author of romantic fantasy. She is the current President of the Science Fiction and Fantasy Writers of America (SFWA) and is a member of Romance Writers of America (RWA), and Novelists, Inc. (NINC). She is best known for her RITA® Award-winning novel, *The Pages of the Mind*, the recent trilogy, *The Forgotten Empires*, and the wildly popular, *Dark Wizard*. Jeffe lives in Santa Fe, New Mexico.

Jeffe can be found online at her website: JeffeKennedy.com, on her podcast First Cup of Coffee, every Sunday at the popular SFF Seven blog, on Facebook, on Goodreads, on BookBub, and pretty much constantly on Twitter @jeffekennedy. She is represented by Sarah Younger of Nancy Yost Literary Agency.

jeffekennedy.com

facebook.com/Author.Jeffe.Kennedy

twitter.com/jeffekennedy

goodreads.com/author/show/1014374.Jeffe_Kennedy

bookbub.com/profile/jeffe-kennedy

Sign up for her newsletter here.

jeffekennedy.com/sign-up-for-my-newsletter

www.ingramcontent.com/pod-product-compliance
Lightning Source LLC
Chambersburg PA
CBHW032236190726
48289CB00007BA/2402